Cover Design & Interior Format
The Killion Group, Inc.
www.thekilliongroupinc.com

You Can't Build a Herd with 4 Steers, Even in Texas

Dixie Cash

CHAPTER 1

HER PULSE RACING, Cassandra Grace Jennings carefully read the letter from a Texas law firm for the fourth time. After she believed she clearly understood what it said, she drew a deep breath and keyed in her sister's phone number.

A growly female voice answered. "What is it?"

"Come over here."

"What? I'm still asleep."

"Ronny, come over here. It's important."

"Have you looked outside? There's a friggin' blizzard going on."

Earlier this morning, Cassie had braved the storm that had moved in yesterday to get to her mailbox and back. "I know that. I've already been outside."

"I worked late last night," Ronny griped, "and that piece of shit in the driveway choked and sputtered all the way home. I don't know if it will even start today. It's supposed to snow and blow all day. I'm off at both my jobs. I wasn't planning on leaving my apartment."

Veronica Denice Jennings, known by all as Ronny, worked as a cashier and jack-of-all-trades at Dollar General in the daytime. On weekends and sometimes weeknights, she tended bar at Duffy's Tavern. With a marshmallow heart, half the time, she spent the extra money she earned as a bartender buying drinks and covering tabs.

As far as Cassie was concerned, instead of getting ahead, Ronny was getting exhausted, with nothing but fatigue to show for her effort.

She sighed. "This can't wait. I need to talk to you face-to-face. I'll go over to your place. I'm on my way."

Cassie bundled up in a thick coat with a fur-lined hood, a wide wool scarf, thick mittens and knee-high boots, her costume for wrestling upstate New York winters. She had done this her whole life. When she and Ronny were children, their mother would bundle them so tightly in layers of clothing they could barely move their arms and legs.

She should be accustomed to the winter's brutality, but every year found her wondering why she put up with it. She didn't ski or ice skate or enjoy winter sports of any kind; her ten-year-old Kia Sorento didn't have snow tires. What she did mostly was trudge back and forth to work at Blueberry Elementary School every weekday where she taught fifth grade, then return home and huddle by a fire until she had to trudge to work again.

She was single. She had no obligations. Why didn't she move to Florida? Or Arizona or California even?

Or Texas.

As she waded through knee-deep snow to her own car in her unplowed driveway, a whistling wind blowing snow against her face, she wondered if her own vehicle would start. Thankfully, the ten-year-old

SUV grumbled to life and she inched over icy roads toward her sister's apartment a few blocks away.

Ronny answered the door with bed hair, raccoon eyes and wearing a raggedy flannel robe. A tiny diamond stud glinted from the side of her nose. She always looked a mess when she first rose from bed, but long and lanky, cleaned up, dressed up and her green eyes made up, she looked like a magazine cover model. Cassie, having inherited their mother's short stature and wholesome look, envied her.

And at the moment, she welcomed the sight of her standing behind the open door offering a shield against the elements and hanging onto a mug of something steaming.

Cassie stamped snow off her boots. "Is that coffee? Got any more?"

"Sure. Come in and help yourself."

Cassie walked into the living room and pushed back the fur-rimmed hood attached to her thick, puffy coat. She untied her wool scarf, neatly folded it and laid it across the sofa arm. Then, she peeled off her mittens and stuffed them into her coat pocket. Finally, she shrugged out of her coat, laid it on top of the scarf on the sofa arm and fluffed her short naturally curly hair.

"All set?" Ronny asked.

"What do you mean?"

"I'm worn out just watching you disrobe. I was wondering what was going to come off next."

"Bite me, Ronny. You know how much I hate this weather."

"Me? I love it. I was thinking I should go ice fishing."

In the corner of the living room stood a six-foot brightly lit, artificial Christmas tree. "Christmas has been over nearly a week," Cassie said to her sister. "You should take that Christmas tree down."

Ronny glanced toward the tree. "I like it. I might leave it up for a month. Those bright lights make me think I'm in Vegas."

"When were you ever in Vegas?"

"I've seen pictures. Besides, maybe it'll lure Santa to drop by and leave me a present he overlooked."

"Hah." Cassie replied, making her way to Ronny's tight galley kitchen. She picked up the coffee carafe, giving its deep brown liquid a jaundiced look. Her sister was known to save coffee and reheat it for days. Cassie poured her mug full and started to sip but halted. "Is this fresh?"

"Well...It was yesterday."

Rolling her eyes, Cassie dumped the coffee down the sink drain. "It's a wonder you don't poison yourself, Ronny."

"What the hell, Cassie? Have you seen the price of coffee? Any old way I can save a buck, I'm there."

Ronny gathered her long hair that hung past the middle of her back into a ponytail, then knotted it and pinned it on top of her head. For the Christmas holidays, she had added green and red streaks to her brown hair. "Why are you over here rattling my cage so early?"

"It's eleven o'clock. That isn't early."

"It is to me. Saturday night. I worked late, remember?"

Cassie whipped the letter out of her purse. "Read this."

Ronny snatched the envelope. "This had better be good. Lord, my eyes are barely open. I'm not sure I can even focus."

Cassie sank to a chair at a small kitchen table while her sister pulled the letter out of its envelope with long, beringed fingers. She wore silver rings on two fingers of each hand.

She read aloud:

"Dear Miz Jenkins. This is to inform you that your father, John Lawton Jennings, has passed. His last will stipulates you and your sister, Veronica Denice Jennings, shall inherit eighty acres of land in Cameron County, Texas, including a 1,200 square foot home and livestock. The location is approximately twelve miles south of the small community of Los Tropicos. Both parties are required to live in the home for one year after which time the deed will be recorded in your names. Please be in touch with me at Atwater and Airedale, Attorneys at Law, to resolve how you wish to handle this inheritance. My email address is paxjatwater@gmail.com. My mailing address is P. O. Box 2854, Harlingen, Texas. You may call me at 776-555-1225. Yours truly, Paxton J. Atwater, Esquire."

Ronny looked up from the letter. "I'll be damn. What's esquire? Is that his name?"

"It's his title. It's what lawyers call themselves."

"Humph. One of my husbands was a lawyer. You'd think I'd know that, but I don't remember hearing *esquire*. Isn't an Airedale a dog?"

Cassie gave her a frown. "I don't know. What difference does it make?"

Ronny's shoulders lifted in a shrug. "Just asking. How big is twelve-hundred square feet anyway?"

"Bigger than my house and my house is bigger than your apartment. So…"

"Did you know the old man bought the farm? He was in Texas?"

"All I know is he was from Texas originally, but I haven't heard from him or heard anything about him since we buried Mom ten years ago. Have you?

Ronny's head shook. "Why would I hear from him? Even if he called or something, I'd probably hang up on him."

"Mom used to keep up with him, though I don't know why."

"Wow," Ronny said, taking a chair adjacent to Cassie's. "We're orphans."

"We've been orphans for years, Ronny. Now, we're heirs. We need to get to Texas."

"You can't be serious. Texas is like a whole other country. For all I know, you need a passport to go there. It's gazillion miles away. It would take years to drive there. And Texans? They're a different breed of people."

"As usual, you exaggerate."

"I'm serious. I've met a few Texans in the bar. They don't talk like we do, think or even eat like we do, but man, they can drink. I think they're all drunks."

"You don't know any of that to be true."

"I know I don't know how to ride a horse and do not intend to learn. And the heat. My God, Cassie. From what I've heard about Texas, the heat alone would outright kill us both. No sir, I am not going to Hell while I'm still alive."

"We have to look into it, at least. I couldn't live

with not knowing what we passed up. We should go down there and take a first-hand look."

"Where is Cameron County, Texas?"

"I looked it up on Google and Wikipedia. It's in what they call South Texas. It's close to the border and—"

"The *Mexican* border?"

"There's only two, Ronny, and we live next door to the northern one."

"People are getting killed down there."

"Not everybody. The biggest town is Harlingen. It looks like a nice town. It's bigger than Tonawilla."

"How would we get there? Neither one of our cars would make it, especially in the wintertime. We'd be lucky to get out of New York. And gasoline. What would that cost?"

Cassie placed her forefinger against her lips. "Hmm. I wonder if we could borrow Frank's Prius?... Probably not, I think he loves that car more than he loves his mother."

"Probably more than he loves you, too."

"That's a mean thing to say."

Ronny shrugged. "Facts are facts, Sister."

Her sister's remark struck a nerve within Cassie, because in her heart of hearts, she suspected it was true. She and Frank Kowalski had been together since high school, had literally grown up together. She waited for years for him to pop the question in a romantic way, but it never happened.

She was the queen of being taken for granted. Over time, their relationship had become more like sister and brother. The promise of what he could become, once gargantuan in Cassie's eyes, had shrunk to the size of a pea.

Oh, he had a decent job as General Manager of Big Tony's Auto Parts. He had the respect of the company's owner and a good relationship with his customers, but he had zero ambition beyond that. He was content with the status quo. In fact, his plan was to work at Big Tony's from now on and live in the town where he was born until he went to his grave in the local cemetery.

"Wonder why that lawyer sent you a letter, but not me," Ronny said.

"He probably couldn't find you. Good grief, you've changed addresses a dozen times and had three name changes."

Ronny waved two fingers back and forth like a pendulum. "Unh-uh. Do not criticize. I've always taken back my maiden name."

"I know, I know. Look, Ronny, we can't just turn our backs on this. I've been thinking about it. We could sell both of our cars and buy one that's newer than ten years old. Then we could drive down there in a reliable car."

"And who gets the car when we come back?"

"Why would we come back to Tonawilla, New York, where it snows five feet every winter? Okay, if we can't drive, we can fly. Call it a vacation. We'll meet with the attorney, look at the property, then decide what to do."

"I couldn't buy an airline ticket if I was going to be shot."

"I have some money left in my Christmas account. I can pay for a couple of airline tickets. Think about it, Ronny. We're inheriting a home in a place they say is warm. A home that we don't have to pay rent on. We have nothing to lose and possibly a lot to gain. It's one year out of our lives, which, by the way, aren't so great."

"Speak for yourself. My life's okay."

"No, it isn't. You're working ridiculous hours at two dead-end jobs. You can do that down there. We don't have family left here."

"We have a cousin in Manhattan."

Their one cousin was an actress who lived in Manhattan. "How often do we see her? She never comes here to visit. The only time we see her is if we go down there and she isn't too busy. All you'd be leaving behind are three divorced husbands, one of whom has threatened to shoot you more than once."

"Oh, well. I need some excitement in my life. Besides, I don't have any vacation time left at Dollar General. I'd have to ask for time off without pay. I don't know if they would agree to that."

"Even if they don't, you don't have to worry about Duffy's," Cassie said. "Mike Duffy says you're the best bartender he's ever had."

"And what about *your* job, Miss Prissy Pants? You're the one with a *career*. She emphasized career with air quotes.

Cassie had been a fifth-grade teacher ever since she graduated from college seven years back. She had never wanted to be anything else. "I'm off until the middle of January. If we decide to stay in Texas, I can still finish out the school year here by remote. Then, I'll get a job as a teacher down there. I'm sure they have schools."

Ronny closed her eyes and pressed her fingers against her temples. "Hell. Just hell. I guess we're going to Texas."

She looked up and shook a finger at Cassie. "But I guarantee you I'm not going to like it." She threw up a hand. "Hell, I'll go up in flames like a struck match. You won't have to cremate me, just mail me home in an envelope."

Cassie laughed. Her big sister had a gift for hyperbole. Usually, unless her dramatic take on any and all things got out of hand, it was entertaining. "I'm going home and get the ball rolling. Stay near your phone, Calamity."

"Calamity is right," Ronny grumbled.

The next morning, Cassie sat in Frank Kowalski's office in Big Tony's Auto Parts squirming in her chair. Outside, a chilling wind howled.

"You cannot truly believe this is a good idea," Frank said for the third time. He stood leaning his bottom against his desk, his arms crossed over his chest. "Are you listening to me? Hello?"

Cassie didn't do well being lectured to and she found it even more unappealing from someone she had come to admire less and less. She feigned being brought to attention by his preaching. "Huh? Oh, sorry. What were you saying?"

"Taking off, leaving everything behind, leaving your job, your house, not to mention me. What's gotten into you?"

"My house is a rental, Frank. I've paid enough rent there to own it, but I never will. Ronny and I have no choice. If we don't go, we forfeit the inheritance and we don't even know for sure what it is. It's only a year, not a lifetime." She gave him a pointed look. "Besides, it isn't like our relationship is going anywhere."

Frank's brown eyes narrowed. "I get it. You're trying to get me to propose."

Cassie sighed. "No, Frank. That is not what I was hinting at. In fact—"

She stopped short of saying what she was thinking: *This relationship is a carousel going round and round and I want a roller coaster.*

Cassie knew for sure the last thing on her mind when she headed for the bright white light would not be "I wish I had…" She wanted to experience it all and right now and a tongue lashing from Frank was not part of her plan.

«Tell you what, Cassie," he went on. "I'll consent for you to go to Texas if you'll promise me one thing.»

Consent? A splinter of anger ignited within Cassie. Her jaw clenched. "What?"

Frank dug a small notebook from his shirt pocket, flipped past a few pages, leaned over his desk and began writing. Finally, he tore the page out of the notebook and handed it to her. "Since you won't see reason, if you decide to stay down there, here are five things you need to think about and work on during our year apart. When you get back, if everything on that list has been taken care of and my mom approves, we'll talk marriage."

Cassie stared down at the small piece of lined paper, then up at him. The fire of rage she seldom experienced roared up her spine and smoldered in her brain. She felt her cheeks flush.

"You're blushing." He giggled and touched his fingertip to her nose. "You look cute."

Cassie wanted to stomp her foot and yell; she wanted to wring Frank Kowalski's neck. She batted his finger away.

He cleared his throat, brought up short by his failing to distract her from her mission. "Okay. I see I'm not getting anywhere. Take that note home and study it. Then, if you're still set on going, Mom and I'll drive you and Ronny to the airport."

Fighting back tears, Cassie rose stiffly from her chair and shoved the list in her purse. "Gee, thanks, Frank."

She pulled on her coat, wrapped her head in her scarf and yanked on her mittens.

Frank lifted his palms, his shoulders scrunched up to his ear lobes. "You're leaving? You didn't say what you think."

"You know what, Frank? I'll get back to you on that. Right now, I'm meeting Ronny for lunch."

Cassie marched toward the door.

Frank chuckled behind her. «One thing I know for sure. Veronica Jennings would never make it in Texas."

Her hand on the doorknob, Cassie turned back. "I doubt if she cares about your opinion."

"She'd never make it," Frank said again. "Even Texas is not big enough for her ego and loud mouth."

As Cassie slammed the door, she heard him say, "It's hot down there, you know."

She carefully picked her steps across the icy parking lot to her SUV and inched the short distance to the busiest café in town, At The Coffee Cup. Ronny waited at a table in a corner. A busy waitress quickstepped over and took their order for hamburgers, left them silverware and napkins.

Cassie tearfully repeated her conversation with Frank to her dumbstruck sister.

"He said that? What the hell does he mean I'd never make it in Texas?"

Seeking to diminish Ronny's histrionics, Cassie patted the air with her palms. "Don't get upset."

"A list? That asshole made a list of stuff for you to work on? Lemme see that list."

Cassie reached into her purse and pulled out the small piece of paper. "I haven't read it yet. Knowing Frank, I really don't want to. Promise me you won't do something that'll only make things worse."

"Give it to me." She snatched the list from Cassie's fingers. Drumming her bright red acrylic nails on the table, she read it in a few seconds.

She raised her eyes and drew a breath through her nose. "That asshole. I never liked him, even when we were kids. …You haven't read it? You should. It's amusing….Learn to cook? I'd say, with all the free meals you've cooked for him while he sits on his ass and watches TV, you cook just fine. Be more organized? You do his laundry and yours both. You clean his apartment on weekends and let your own house go? Not to mention helping—"

"Ronny, stop."

"Oh, hell, I can't go on without my head exploding

anyway. But I'll add this. Apparently, you need to lose ten pounds and be more affectionate."

"Ten pounds? *Huh.* Like he'd notice. Be more affectionate? What does that even mean?"

"I think he's talking about sex, Cassie."

Cassie had never slept with another man. She knew only that part of her relationship with Frank was far from perfect. She had never heard bells ring or seen lights flashing in the way she had read about in romance novels.

Her cheeks warmed and she ducked her chin. "Oh, I see."

"God, I don't know when I've been madder," Ronny growled.

Uh-oh. Now her sister was on a tear. "Ronny," Cassie said, "calm down."

Ronny pawed in her oversize satchel and came up with a pen, then grabbed a napkin. "Let me just make a list for Mr. Frank Kowalski. Is that okay with you?"

"Be my guest."

Ronny began writing feverishly, pausing occasionally to think before continuing. Finally, she slapped the napkin on the table in front of Cassie. "There. Promise me you'll give him this and I don't give a damn who he thinks wrote it."

Cassie held the napkin at an angle and began reading:

Number One, add a couple of inches to your dick.

Giggling, Cassie covered her mouth with her fingers. After three husbands, Ronny was bound to know more about that subject than she did.

"Eh?" Ronny asked.

Still blushing, Cassie looked up at her sister.

"I'm serious, Cassie. I've always suspected he was an inch or two or even three shy."

"Is that possible?"

Ronny rolled her eyes. "You're unbelievable. Read the rest of it."

Cassie returned to the list:

Two, get a personality.

Three, get a job with a salary higher than your IQ.

Four, jump up and kiss my ass as I fly off to Texas.

And I don't need a ride to the airport from you and your mother.

Cassie couldn't keep from chuckling. "You nail it every time, Ronny. I'm going back to Big Tony's and hand it to Frank directly."

"Don't worry, Sis. I'll take care of you. I've got your New York ass." Ronny raised a high-five palm to her sister.

Cassie slapped her palm. "Texas, here we come."

CHAPTER 2

Two weeks later
Harlingen, Texas.....

JUST BEFORE NOON on a January day, Cassie and Ronny's small jet airliner landed on an airstrip in Harlingen, Texas. For twelve hours they had been either airborne or getting on or getting off airplanes.

They'd had a layover in Chicago where they had been frozen de-boarding; they slept briefly in the chairs in the waiting area. They had then been delayed by ice but finally boarded a different plane to Dallas. They'd had another layover in Dallas waiting for a flight to Harlingen.

Flying versus driving. The debate had gone on for days. In the end, they concluded if they decided to accept the inheritance and stay in Texas, they could return to Tonawilla and rent a U-Haul for their stuff.

Meanwhile, Frank and his mother had agreed to let them both park their cars at his mother's house.

"Nope, not doing that," Ronny had said, shaking her head. "I don't trust them. Mike Duffy lives on five acres. He said I could park at his house. He's got a shed he isn't using."

A rich baritone voice came over the loudspeaker system, interrupting Cassie's thoughts. "Good morning, ladies and gentlemen. This is your pilot speaking. The time in Harlingen, Texas is eleven-fifteen a.m. The temperature is a comfortable ninety-one degrees…" Blah, blah, blah…

"*Jesus Christ*," Ronny stage whispered. "Did you hear what the pilot just said? Did you?"

"I wasn't paying attention," Cassie answered. "It's just going to feel so good to stand." She got to her feet and squeezed herself into the aisle; reached into the overhead storage to claim her carry-on suitcase.

Ronny followed her. "He said 'it's a comfortable ninety-one degrees.' The last time I was in that kind of weather I was lathered in sunscreen and had a tropical drink in my hand."

Cassie had seen the pictures a few years back when Ronny and her third husband had honeymooned in the Bahamas.

"I knew it," Ronny went on. "I'm going to burn the fuck up."

Swathed in a veil of sweat herself, Cassie felt as if she were trapped in a sauna. She was sure her hair was starting to frizz around her perspiring hairline. She was also exhausted and in no mood for her sister's drama. "Ronny, people can hear you."

"We're going to stay here a year?" Ronny railed. "*Hah!* What will the temperature be in July or August?"

Cassie wiped her brow with the back of her hand. "It probably wouldn't hurt to get out of some of these heavy clothes."

"Good idea. I look like Nanook of the North and

you know what I'm wearing under this heavy coat? More winter clothes. And why do I have on all these winter clothes? Because you told me to wear layers. I thought you checked out the weather app."

"I did, but I assumed it was a typo. I couldn't believe it was really this warm. It was minus-two at home."

"You're right about one thing. We've got to get out of these clothes. The pom-pom on top of my beanie hat is melting."

Cassie rolled her eyes. Sometimes her sister's meltdowns were too much.

They inched forward to de-plane. Once in the terminal they began shedding their coats and sweaters and broke in to peals of laughter. "Everyone is staring at us," Ronny managed to say between guffaws.

"I can't blame them," Cassie said, wiping a tear of mirth from her eye. "They think we're crazy. Down here, they might not even know what a wool sweater is. Let's find a restroom and then get our luggage. And we need to find the car rental. We still have a two-hour drive ahead of us."

Rolling a small carry-on bag and fanning herself with one hand as they walked toward baggage claim, Ronny muttered, "Remind me that if I ever want to kill an ex, I've found the perfect place to dispose of the body."

Cassie managed only a weak smile. She was desperate for the inheritance to be a positive event in their lives. To pay for the plane tickets and support herself and Ronny during this trip, she had cleaned out her savings account as well as her Christmas account. The only assets she had left were a worn-out car and a return ticket to Tonawilla, New York.

Sure enough, Ronny's boss at Dollar General had not been willing to allow her to just take a week or two off, even without pay. If they decided to return to Tonawilla, Cassie would still have her teaching job, but the only job Ronny would have was tending bar part-time at Duffy's Tavern.

Mike Duffy had told her he would hold her job for her for a little while, but not forever. It didn't matter. Ronny didn't make enough tending bar part-time to support herself.

Something encouraging needed to happen soon.

Now they stood in front of a tall desk at a car rental kiosk looking out the window into the parking lot at a ridiculously small car. A young Hispanic woman behind the desk spoke in such broken English Cassie thought she had misunderstood. "You can't be serious," Cassie said.

"That car's smaller than a golf cart," Ronny carped.

"Iz Smart Car," the clerk replied. "You ax for sheap."

Cassie looked at the stack of their suitcases, most of which were Ronny's, then back at the tiny car. "I know, but this is a smaller vehicle than what I expected. I don't think our luggage will fit."

"No worry, *chica*. Efrain make fit. He do all time."

She gestured toward a small Hispanic man standing by with his wrists crossed behind his back. "*Si,*" he said, nodding and grinning.

"I also asked for GPS," Cassie said.

"No worry. It has."

In half an hour and a flurry of activity, Efrain, using a variety of tie downs, bungee cords and rope, had all the luggage secured to the top, sides and back of the toy car.

"See?" he said, obviously proud. "Easy peasy." Gesturing with his hands and arms, he spoke in a string of Spanish. "*Me aseguré de que las bolsas estuvieran colocadas correctamente para que el auto no se vuelque.*" He ended with making a tipping motion with both hands.

"What the hell did he say?" Ronny asked, wide-eyed.

Cassie was thankful she had taken conversational Spanish in college. "I think he said he fixed it so the car doesn't tip over."

"Tip over?" Ronny squeaked, her voice an octave higher than normal. "It looks like it could roll, like a big ball with eyes."

Giving up was all Cassie could think to do. A larger vehicle would have cost more money. "*Gracias,*" she said to the Hispanic man, then turned to her sister. "Let's just...just get in."

"Are you sure it's safe?"

"Of course it is. Ronny, get in." Cassie squeezed behind the wheel. "Oh, no," she mumbled. "The brake is the size of a half dollar."

Ronny finally slid onto the passenger seat. With her long legs, her knees almost touched her chin. "It's a good thing you know a little Spanish."

"A little is right," Cassie said.

"What if the roof caves in?"

"Ronny, give it a rest. We need to contact that attorney and let him know we've arrived."

"Okay, but can we get something to eat first? I'm starving."

"You should have eaten what they offered on the plane. It wasn't half bad."

"I never eat something when there's a high probability I could see it again."

"You'd think you'd have outgrown motion sickness by now."

Ronny shrugged. "I might have, but I haven't had the nerve to test it. Anyway, find a fast-food drive-up or something, I don't want to go inside somewhere and leave our luggage in a parking lot."

"I don't know if this car will fit in a fast-food lane, but I guess we can try." Cassie pressed in, "closest fast-food restaurant" on the GPS and several addresses popped up on the screen. "Looks like it's tacos. We've got Taco Mucho, Taco Fiesta or Taco Time."

"What if I don't want a taco?" Ronny muttered. "What if I want, oh, let's say, a pizza. Any pizza addresses?"

"Look," Cassie said in the calmest voice she could muster. "I know you like tacos. Duffy's has tacos on Tuesday night. You make them and you love them. You've even brought some home. Let's just get something to eat and call the attorney. I'm exhausted."

"Fine," Ronny said petulantly. "I'll do tacos."

Following GPS instructions, they soon reached Taco Fiesta. Concrete curbs separated two narrow lanes guiding them to the electronic ordering robots.

"I don't know about this," Cassie said, steering the small round car into one of the lanes, checking in the side mirrors to make sure their luggage wasn't obstructing the neighboring lane. At the speaker box to give their order, she saw a sign: OUT OF ORDER. GO TO WINDOW.

She eased toward the order window, pulling as close as she dared.

"Don't forget I don't do gluten," Ronny said.

Cassie sighed. Eating gluten-free was a new "thing" with her big sister.

A teenage Hispanic girl appeared in the window and slid it open, a bored expression on her face. "I can help you?"

"Yes," Cassie answered. "Do you have gluten-free taco shells?"

"*Mi abuela* make the shells by hand. Sixty years she make the shells. She no add gluten."

Cassie turned to Ronny. "The taco shells are handmade. Are you sure you have to have gluten-free?"

Ronny leaned forward and looked upward at the order taker, "Are they corn? I can have corn."

"We don' sell corn. Shells are *masa*," the order taker said.

"*Masa* is corn," Cassie told her sister in a low voice, then turned back to the order taker. "That's okay." She searched for the menu. "I don't see your menu."

"We haf beef taco, shrimp taco, chicken taco, goat taco—"

"Did you say goat?" Ronny asked. "*Blech!*"

"We'll have two shrimp tacos and two chicken," Cassie said quickly, before her sister went off on a tangent.

The teenager keyed in the order. "You wan' somet'ing to drink?"

"We'll have two medium Cokes."

"Haf only small and extra-large."

"Extra-large is fine."

"What kind?"

"Coke," Cassie said in a louder voice.

"What kind? We haf Dr. Pepper, Diet Dr. Pepper, Mountain Dew, Pepsi, *Jarritos* Pineapple, *Jarritos* Mango, *Jarritos* Fruit Punch…"

Cassie looked at Ronny. "Dr. Pepper?"

"They don't have just plain old Coke?"

"Apparently not. Ronny, just choose something."

Ronny shrugged.

Cassie turned back to the teenager. "Dr. Pepper. Make it Dr. Pepper."

"Okay. You wan' diet Dr. Pepper, Cherry Dr. Pepper, Cream Soda Dr. Pep—"

Cassie was losing patience. Maybe that speaker wasn't broken after all. Maybe it had just given up. "Just regular Dr. Pepper, please," she said peevishly.

"Any hot sauce? We haf *caliente, mucho caliente*—"

"No, thank you," Cassie interrupted.

"Yeah," Ronny said. "I don't think we should venture down that road."

In a few minutes, the teenager handed the order through the window—a cardboard tray holding two small brown paper bags showing grease spots, a dozen napkins and two drinks the size of the car. Cassie handed the whole thing to Ronny.

"This must be extra-large," Ronny quipped. "I'd hate to think it's medium."

"You heard her. They do not have medium. I'm going to pull over into the parking lot and we can eat and call the lawyer."

She lifted her foot off the tiny brake pedal, intending to slowly round the corner of the building. Accidentally, her foot missed the brake and floored the gas pedal. The car leaped forward. Cassie slammed on the brake with a loud *screek*.

A heavy metal sign hanging from the corner of the building caught in a bungee cord holding two of their suitcases in place on top of the car and snapped it. The suitcases flew off the car and hit the ground. They popped open and clothing scattered over the parking lot.

The drinks in Ronny's hands had jolted and poured two quarts of liquid all over Ronny's front. "Shit!" she shrieked.

Cassie slapped both palms against her cheeks. "Oh, my gosh! I am so sorry, Ronny."

But Ronny had already jumped out of the car and was picking up clothing and muttering cusswords.

Behind them a car horn *beep-beeped*. Ronny turned to face it, made a fist and bent her arm in the universal sign of "up yours."

An Hispanic man stuck his head out the window and yelled a stream of Spanish.

"Hey, buster! Can you just wait a minute?" Ronny yelled back.

The whole upper half of the Hispanic man's body came out the driver's window with his hands free and his two middle fingers thrust in the air. Another string of Spanish came out of his mouth.

Ronny stuck her head back through the small car's passenger side window and said to Cassie, "What did he say?"

"Something about stupid gringo women."

"*That* is racist. Not only is it racist, it's sexist."

"Ronny, don't go there."

"How are we going to get all this stuff attached to this car again? Get out and help me."

Cassie squeezed from behind the steering wheel, at a loss where to start. The Hispanic man continued his diatribe. Ronny turned back to him and cussed at him in a stream of English words Cassie had never heard.

She closed her eyes and shook her head. Ronny used to be a nice girl, but her personality had coarsened since she had gone to work in Duffy's Tavern, which was frequented by mostly men.

A Taco Fiesta employee came outside and began to help. Horns honked, people yelled from their cars behind them. Cars attempted to turn around in the narrow lanes and became stuck.

Just then, a siren blasted. A police cruiser stopped in front of Taco Fiesta. Cassie's breath caught. *Oh, no. We're going to be arrested.*

A cop got out and ambled over to where she and Ronny were standing, their hands and arms full of underwear. The bun that had started out on top of Ronny's head had become a ponytail hanging down one side of her face.

The cop looked around. "You ladies having trouble?"

"I am so sorry, officer," Cassie said. "At the car rental place at the airport, an employee strapped our luggage on the car with bungee cords and that sign up there"—she pointed up to the metal sign on the corner of the building—"tore them loose. And we don't have any more bungee cords or anything." Tears burned her eyes. Any minute she was going to cry.

Without a word, the cop spoke into his shoulder mic, then walked back to his cruiser, opened the trunk and brought out rope. He came back and with the help of the Taco Fiesta employee, worked at tying the suitcases back to the car with rope.

Meanwhile, the girl taking orders at the window came outside with a tablet and car by car, began writing down orders.

Another police cruiser came to a stop behind the first one and another cop got out. He walked over to the fast-food lane and began sorting out the chaos. He even put two people in handcuffs.

An hour later, their suitcases had been re-secured by ropes. Cassie and Ronnie slid back into the toy car. "I think that does it," the cop said. "You ladies take care and have a nice day." He directed them out to the street.

Cassie stopped on the side of the road before pulling into the street traffic and pressed her forehead against the steering wheel. "Oh, my gosh, Ronny. I thought we were going to be arrested."

"You know what? If they've got an air-conditioned cell, I don't even give a damn."

"I'm worn-out," Cassie said.

"I'm hot," Ronny said. "Let's get going. Pretty soon, flies are going to start collecting on my sugar-soaked clothes."

Cassie pressed the town of Los Tropicos into the GPS and away they went.

CHAPTER 3

MORE THAN AN hour later and midafternoon, Cassie stopped at the edge of a town at a narrow rectangular green sign that announced, "Los Tropicos" in white letters. A few old buildings—most with boarded up windows—stood on the sides of the paved road that stretched out and away as far as the eye could see. No human being could be seen. Only a few dogs.

"Damn," Ronny said. "Is this it? Are you sure that GPS was right?"

"It's a small town, Ronny. Google said a hundred thirty-six people."

"Los Tropicos, my ass. *Lost* Tropicos is more like it."

"Look, there's a gas pump and a grocery store. Oh, look, there's a sign that says, 'café' on that post in front of the grocery store. There's everything we need."

"The essentials of life. I'm hungry. I don't see a lawyer's office. Let's go to the café and eat."

"You've got the letter. His phone number is on it. Call him."

Ronny dug the fateful letter out of her satchel, pressed in the number and put the phone on

"Speaker." A twangy male voice answered on the third burr. "Atwater and Airedale. Paxton J. Atwater speaking."

Ronny explained who she was.

"That's great. You're just across the road from the city park. Just go over to the park and stay right there. I'll be there in about ten minutes."

Ronny disconnected. "I don't see a park."

"I see some trees. Are those palm trees?"

"Yep. I'm going to take off another layer." Ronny opened the door and scooted out, pulled her Dr. Pepper soaked, cable-knit sweater over her head. "Oh, my God, Cassie. It is so warm."

"Get back in the car. I'm going to park over there by those trees."

Minutes later, an old faded red, rattle-trap pickup truck pulling a travel trailer veered off the road and stopped beside them. A huge pair of cow horns that stretched from fender to fender was mounted on the grill.

"What the hell?" Ronny said. "Are those real cow's horns on the front of that pickup? Is that a camper trailer it's pulling? It is. And a crappy-looking one at that."

"I know," Cassie said and bit down on her lower lip.

A scrawny small man stepped out of the pickup truck and walked toward them. He wore a short sleeve shirt with snap buttons, an odd-looking tie and denim jeans. The legs of his jeans were stuffed inside the tops of red cowboy boots and huge hat sat on his head.

Cassie's gaze zeroed in on the pistol strapped to his

belt. Short of cops, she had never seen anyone wear a gun. "He's wearing a gun," she said, *sotto voce.*

"I heard they do that down here," Ronny said, in an equally low voice. "Is that hat what they call a sombrero?"

"I think so," Cassie answered. She nervously buzzed down the window.

"Howdy," the man said, pushing his hat back with his thumb. "You must be the Jennings sisters. My name's Paxton J. Atwater. Welcome to Los Tropicos, Texas."

Sitting on the ground on its haunches, its tongue lolling, a panting tan and black dog at least three feet tall looked up at Cassie.

"This here's my partner," Mr. Atwater said. "He's an Airedale and that's what I named him. Atwater and Airedale, get it?" He huh-huh-huhed at his own joke. "And how was your trip?"

"Long," Ronny answered.

"Yes, it was very tiring."

"I'm hungry," Ronny said.

"Well, then, let's get this paperwork taken care of so you ladies can get something to eat and rest." Mr. Atwater walked back to the trailer, opened the door and let the dog go inside. He motioned for them to come in.

"I told you an Airedale was a dog," Ronny whispered loudly. "I don't like the looks of this."

Cassie unfastened her seat belt. "Come on. Get out. We've come this far."

They climbed the travel trailer's narrow steps into a surprisingly well-furnished office. The interior was refreshingly cool, thanks to a small air conditioner mounted in a window. It emitted a low hum. A desk, small but expensive-looking, and three chairs were all the furniture the small space would hold.

Three diplomas, doubled matted and framed, hung on the wall behind it. Good grief, Mr. Atwater had a pedigree education.

"Oh, my gosh," Cassie said. "You went to Harvard?"

Mr. Atwater smiled. "Sure did. Bet you thought I graduated from an online college and never left Texas. Truth is, I did leave Texas, but as the old saying goes, I got back here as quick as I could. I was born and raised in Harlingen, Texas."

Cassie quailed, having her inner thoughts so raw and exposed. In an effort to change the subject she said, "So this is your office. A mobile legal office. That's…well, it's unusual."

"It's practical, too. Most of my clients have transportation difficulties so I go to them. Saves time and money and it's a good tax write off."

"That's wonderful. You must be either rich or a great humanitarian."

"Yeah," Ronny put in. "From the looks of things around here, there couldn't be that much money in cases you have to go to."

"Veronica!" Cassie snapped. "That's rude."

Ronny's brow raised. "I'm just saying."

"It's okay," Mr. Atwater said, still smiling. "Remember in your fine state of New York about ten years ago when a high school teacher was accused of exchanging a passing grade for sex with six students?"

"I remember that," Cassie said. "I'm a teacher myself. We studied his case in one of my classes. His name was Hanson or something like that."

"That's right. Robert Hanson. He was found guilty and spent eight years in prison. His life was ruined. His wife left him. His children turned their backs on him. He lost everything, but he never gave up his steadfast claim of innocence.

"I took his appeal for court practice and proved him innocent. Those sweet students had made up the whole story and one of them even admitted it. I got him out of prison, but he was still registered as a sex offender.

"In a civil suit that followed, I won him forty-six million dollars, due to wrongful prosecution, mental anguish and loss of income. My portion of the settlement was…let's say, substantial. I'm in a position to be selective what cases I take. Don't let anyone tell you being rich sucks."

He rounded the end of the desk, pulled his pistol from its holster and laid it on the desk, then sat down behind it in an expensive-looking leather chair. "You ladies have a seat."

Cassie and Ronny exchanged glances, then timidly eased down into the chairs in front of the desk.

"Now, which one of you is which?"

Cassie spoke up. "I'm Cassie." She gestured toward Ronny. "And this is my sister Ronny."

Mr. Atwater opened a drawer and produced a sheaf of papers. "Let's go over your daddy's will."

He handed the papers to Cassie. She read, then passed each page to Ronny.

Cassie was too nervous to absorb the details of the lengthy document. Thankfully, Mr. Atwater said, "To be clear and summarize, the house has to be lived in for one year from the date you sign these papers. After a year, the four cattle can be sold but not before. So, if you stick it out a year and take care of those cows, the property in its entirety will belong to the two of you. Or the one of you that doesn't return to New York. If neither one of you stays here, the property is to be sold and the money donated to ASPCA."

Cassie's pulse had begun to race. She looked at Ronny. Ronny looked back at her, then back at the lawyer. "What's ASPCA?"

"American Society for the Prevention of Cruelty to Animals." Without missing a beat, the lawyer continued, "Also, there's a pickup truck. It's a collector's item, but it runs. John drove it every day. In addition, I have a key to a safe deposit box at Texas Bank & Loan in Harlingen. At the end of the year, the contents of the safe deposit box will become yours."

"What's in it?" Ronny asked.

"I'm not at liberty to say, Miz Jennings."

Mr. Atwater opened the desk drawer again, pulled out a brown envelope and handed it across the desk. "Meanwhile, here's cash your daddy left to cover what you girls have been out getting here and your living expenses for a time. He knew you might want to bring the house up to *female* standards. He was a bachelor. He lived a minimalist lifestyle."

Ronny reached for the envelope and peeked inside. Without a word, she sat for a full minute staring into it, then passed it to Cassie with a trembling hand.

Cassie reached inside and pulled out a thick stack of bills. Hundred-dollar bills. She gulped. "Is this real money?"

"Absolutely," Mr. Atwater answered.

"Why—why…I—I don't know what to say."

"How much money is this?" Ronny asked.

"Twenty thousand dollars."

Ronny gasped. "You're shittin' me."

Cassie drew a quick breath. She had never seen twenty-thousand dollars in cash and she was sure her sister hadn't either. She almost felt faint. She fanned herself.

"No, ma'am, I am not," Mr. Atwater said.

Ronny's eyes narrowed. "Cool, but we can't live for a year on twenty thousand dollars."

"I understand. Your daddy wanted you to earn what you're inheriting You might have to seek employment."

"Where?" Ronny asked. "This is barely a town."

"I've spoken to the owner of the grocery store and the little café on your behalf. Either or both of you might find jobs there."

Smiling, Mr. Atwater interlocked his fingers and rested them on the desk. "So, ladies, do we have a couple of signatures for me to notarize?"

Cassie looked at her sister, "I'm signing, Ronnie."

Ronny lifted a defiant chin. "Well, I'm not. I'm not signing anything until I've seen the house. My apartment in Tonawilla might not be The Ritz, but it's got a good roof and running water. Show me the house."

"Very astute young lady," Mr. Atwater said, raising his forefinger. "I'd expect nothing less. Okay then, go get in your mobile piece of luggage and follow me." He chuckled, obviously pleased with his attempt at humor. He opened the trailer door, motioned for Airedale to follow him and stepped outside.

Cassie felt so weak in the knees she wondered

if she could stand, much less walk. Even Ronny had nothing smart aleck to say. They followed Mr. Atwater out of the cool trailer into the waning, but hot, afternoon.

As they walked shoulder to shoulder toward the Smart Car, Ronny asked in a whispery voice, "What does astute mean?"

"It means he thinks you're no dummy."

"Humph," Ronny said.

Inside the car, fastening her seatbelt and releasing a great sigh, Cassie said, "I feel like I'm in a fairy tale. I nearly fainted when he said how much money is in that envelope. What do you suppose is in the safe deposit box?"

"More money?"

"My stomach feels like butterflies are swarming in it."

"Butterflies," Ronny said. "Butterflies would be a blessing. I think I'm about to hurl."

"There isn't enough room in this car for you to hurl. Don't let that money get lost in that satchel you call a purse."

Ronnie hugged the bag closer to her chest. "I got it. Come on. Let's light this candle."

Mr. Atwater climbed back into the pickup truck, fired the engine and headed south. Cassie followed. They soon turned off the paved highway and bumped along a flat dirt road, swerving this way and that to avoid potholes.

"This looks like a desert," Ronny griped. "What happened to the orchards and palm trees around that town of Harlingen?"

"I don't know," Cassie answered, looking around

and at the same time concentrating on following the pickup and trailer that were churning up a cloud of dust. "I thought deserts were supposed to have cactuses and sagebrush. This is worse."

"Hell, he's probably lost," Ronny said. "I sure am."

Suddenly Cassie hit a bump and Ronny's head banged against the tiny car's roof. "*Shit!*" she cried. "We going to be killed getting to this place."

Finally, the motor home's left turn signal light started blinking red. Still following, Cassie bumped and rumbled over several long metal pipes in the ground.

"What the hell was that?" Ronny wailed, her brow tented in a frown. "That loosened all my teeth."

"Those were steel pipes," Cassie answered. "Surely they have a purpose in the middle of the road, but I'm stumped as for what."

While she pondered, Mr. Atwater's pickup came to a halt and Cassie almost rear-ended the travel trailer. The lawyer scooted out, a toothy grin plastered on his face. "Well"—he spread his arms wide-- "here you are!"

"Here we are what?" Cassie asked, ducking out of the toy car. She saw no house.

Ronny followed. Planting her fists on her hips, she wasted no time, opinion or voice. "Okay buddy, if this is some kind of ploy to get us away from town and rob us, you picked the wrong girls. We may not be Texans with a gun in every pocket and purse but we are New Yorkers and we'll cut you! That's right, we'll carve you like a Thanksgiving turkey!"

Cassie stared at her sister in disbelief then swung her gaze back to the attorney who was white as a sheet.

"We will do nothing of the sort, Mr. Atwater. We're both just tired and a little surprised. We thought there was a house."

Mr. Atwater pulled a handkerchief from his rear pocket and dabbed at his forehead. "No apologizes necessary. I forgot y'all probably aren't used to having land. This is just the edge of your property. You can't see your house from here. It's a little further south. In fact, it's only a few feet from the Rio Grande."

"As in river?" Ronny asked.

"Oh, no," Cassie said. "I didn't realize the border was so close to us. Is it dangerous to be here? I mean, I follow the news. I know about the chaos along the Texas-Mexico border." She glanced around.

"People are being killed left and right on the border," Ronny declared. "Do we have the wall? I heard about a wall and—"

"Ma'am, I knew your daddy," Mr. Atwater said, as if he were speaking to one of Cassie's fifth graders. "He wouldn't do anything to harm you. There are over twelve hundred miles of Texas-Mexican border. Twelve hundred.

"The stories of atrocities in some areas are true, but not for the entire twelve hundred miles. Here, we have good relations with our neighbors, *all* our neighbors. The wall was not completed and your home looks out on the river. I, myself, find it lovely. But if you two don't want to stay after the year, I won't have any trouble selling this property." He turned walked back toward the motor home. "Follow me to your house."

Cassie and her sister re-boarded the small car, Cassie's pride smarting from what he had said. "He must think we're stupid women incapable of staying the year here. Ronny, if we have to reinvent ourselves and forget everything we ever knew we're going to stay here a year."

Ronny slid a sideways look at her. "Speak for yourself, Sister. I'm saving any commitments until after we've seen the house. If it's like what we've seen so far, we won't even need to unpack."

CHAPTER 4

FOR ANOTHER FIFTEEN minutes that felt like hours Cassie and her sister followed the attorney's pickup and trailer. Twilight had descended upon them. Apprehension grew by the second within Cassie. She could hear her heartbeat in her ears.

Soon, through the dust cloud kicked up by the attorney's vehicles, she thought she made out outline of a box or something resembling a house. "Look, I think we're here."

Ronny shifted in her seat, trying to sit more upright to see, but her posture was restricted by the car's roof. "That's a house? That looks like pictures I've seen of the Alamo in history books. And it's orange."

Cassie didn't know what was more astounding, the fact her sister was right or that she had cracked a history book. As she remembered her older sister's school years, education had been an afterthought. Boys had unrelentingly been her focus.

Mr. Atwater stepped out of the pickup and walked back to the small car. "After you ladies called and said you were coming, I took the liberty of having the electricity turned on. There was a small fee, but you can pay me back later. I'll go inside and make sure no snakes or any other varmints have taken up residence."

"Snakes?" Cassie asked feebly.

"Wait a minute," Ronnie said. "Nobody said anything about snakes."

But Mr. Atwater had already disappeared behind a primitive-looking door.

Ronnie crossed her arms over her chest. "Snakes in the house? Cassie, I repeat, nobody said anything about snakes."

"I'm sure he's just being cautious." Cassie said. "He's looking out for us."

The door opened, Atwater appeared and motioned them inside. They left the car and passed through the doorway into a small yard. Under the canopy of a tall palm tree stood a dry fountain adorned with a large angel in the center, a wrought-iron table and two chairs.

"What the hell?" Ronny said. "Where's the house?"

"This is a courtyard," Mr. Atwater said. "This is the way Spaniards used to build houses."

"How old is this place?" Cassie asked, looking around wide-eyed.

"Oh, it's at least a hundred years old. It used to be part of a larger estate, but eighty acres is all that's left."

He looked at Ronny. "So, do we get Veronica's signature or am I taking you back to the airport in Harlingen? Sun's going down and I don't like traveling these roads after dark."

"Ah-hah!" Ronny said. "I knew it. It's not even safe enough to drive after dark. Cassie we're leaving, I know you signed but I'm not letting you stay in the armpit of the USA, if we're even still in the USA."

"Ma'am, my goodness," Mr. Atwater said. "How you northern people do go on. I don't drive at night because I'm night blind. I'd drive into the Rio Grande for sure."

Ronny ignored Mr. Atwater's explanation. "Where's that return ticket? I think I want to use it."

Cassie sighed. "Ronny, please. Mom died and left us nothing. She had nothing to leave us. Do you really want to give up half of the only inheritance you'll ever get and go back to Tonawilla and live in a rented apartment the rest of your life? We can make this work if we stay together. There's nothing we can't do together. I'm no good without you and you'd miss me and you know it."

Ronnie wiped a tear from her eye. "Okay, dammit, I'll sign. But if you think I'm going to ignore any and every opportunity to remind you what a big mistake this is, you're crazy."

"Atta girl," Mr. Atwater said. He placed his briefcase on the primitive dining table and produced the document. Ronny signed. He stamped it with the notary seal and tucked it back in his briefcase.

"Now then," he said. "Let me give you a brief tour. There's a little bit of furniture and a few dishes and some pots and pans."

Cassie looked around. She saw a tattered sofa and one lamp. Covering almost all of one wall was the biggest fireplace she had ever seen. "Oh, my gosh. You could build a really big fire in that fireplace."

"Oh, that hasn't been used in years," Mr. Atwater said. "I don't know what shape it's in. I don't recall

John ever having a fire. I wouldn't use it if I were you."

No wall separated the living room from the kitchen. From where she stood in the middle of the living room, Cassie saw a small square cookstove like Ronny had in her apartment back in Tonawilla. Also, a small refrigerator, the badly used square table and two straight backed chairs.

"There's two bedrooms," Mr. Atwater said, "but only one bed. John lived here by himself, so this was all he needed. You'll have to add what you want to make it suit you. That's what that cash is for but spend it frugally."

He walked into the kitchen and pointed out a coffeemaker. "I bought you a new Mr. Coffee and some coffee. You like coffee, don't you?"

"We live for coffee."

"I also bought you a few groceries." He walked over and opened the refrigerator door and revealed eggs and a package of bacon, a package of lunchmeat, a jar of mayonnaise and a package of tortillas. "This should be enough to tide you over until you get back to Harlingen to shop."

"That's forty-five miles," Cassie said. "We just came from there."

Ronny's eyes bugged. "*My God.* You mean we have to drive forty-five miles to buy food?"

Palms open, Mr. Atwater's shoulders shrugged. "Yes, ma'am. In an emergency, you'll find a few things in the little grocery store in town, but you'll have better luck in Harlingen."

Cassie perused the few items in the refrigerator

more closely. "Hm. Guess we'll have to get by on lunchmeat. We don't eat bacon."

Mr. Atwater studied her a few seconds. "You don't eat bacon? Is it a religious thing?"

"No. Our mother thought it was unhealthy and it's expensive."

The attorney pushed his hat back with his thumb and chuckled. "Well, ma'am, around here, if you don't eat bacon, you're in for a world of hurt. Just about every prepared meal in Texas starts with bacon, either the strip itself or the drippings from it."

"I don't see any bread," Ronny said. "If we're going to live on lunchmeat, how are we going to make sandwiches?"

Mr. Atwater picked up a package of tortillas.

Ronny gaped. "We supposed to make a sandwich with lunchmeat and a tortilla?"

"You don't eat tortillas, either?"

"I've never eaten a tortilla in my life except in a taco."

Next, Ronny would be asking about gluten. Cassie jumped in to end a conversation her sister could carry on all night. "We both appreciate all you've done, Mr. Atwater. We'll figure it out."

He smiled. "I know you will. You're smart ladies. You remind me of my mama. She came from a lengthy line of pioneering Texas women, stronger than bleach. She taught me that you don't know what you can conquer until you do it."

"We'll see," Ronnie said, the two words laced with sarcasm.

"Before I leave you," Mr. Atwater said. "I want to make a small suggestion. Leave your lights on at night and be sure to lock your doors. Sometimes we get travelers on foot through these parts and you don't want to make them think this place is vacant."

"What difference does it make if it's vacant?" Ronny asked.

Cassie began to tremble. Only now was she beginning to realize she and Ronny might be in danger. "Oh, my gosh. You're talking about illegal border crossers, aren't you?"

"Yes, ma'am. They're usually hungry and thirsty, so—" Atwater lifted his shoulders in a shrug.

"You mean they'd break in?" Cassie said.

"Oh, my God," Ronny wailed. "Leave it to a father we never knew to give us an inheritance we have to earn in a fuckin' war zone. We're going to be murdered in our sleep."

"What about those pipes we drove over?" Cassie asked. "Aren't those supposed to keep people out?"

"The cattleguard? No, darlin', that's meant to keep animals in. Any human can walk across it."

He continued, as if Ronny were not about to go off like a rocket. "There's one more thing. If you go outside, you might take a stick with you and make some noise. If snakes hear you coming, they'll run from you, but if you surprise one, you might have a problem."

Cassie said. "Snakes have ears?"

Ronny covered her face with both hands and wailed, "I can't believe this."

"Also, we're expecting a little cold front to move in tonight," Mr. Atwater said. "Won't get too cold though and won't last long."

"How cold?" Cassie asked.

"Oh, I've seen it get down as low as thirty-two when one of these fronts moves through."

Ronny flapped her hand at him. "Piece of cake. I go sunbathing when it's thirty-two."

"Well, I don't," Cassie said.

"I put sheets on the bed," Mr. Atwater said, "but I couldn't find a blanket. Guess you can use your coats to keep warm.,"

"If there's anything we're used to, it's cold weather," Cassie said.

Mr. Atwater opened his briefcase again and produced a key ring holding multiple keys. "This here is a key to the house, front and back doors. Also a key to the barn out back. Also a key to the truck."

"Wow," Cassie said. "We have a barn?"

He laid the keyring on the table. "Yes, ma'am. It's not very big. The truck I told you about is parked inside it and there's a little bit of hay to feed the cows."

"And, pray tell, where are the cows?" Ronny asked.

"Somewhere on this property. They graze. But they still need a little bite of hay."

Atwater left. For a few minutes, the silence he left behind was deafening.

"I'm hungry," Ronny said. "We didn't get to eat our tacos back at Taco Fiesta." Ronny opened the refrigerator door, pulled out the package of lunchmeat and the package of tortillas. "Want a gourmet sandwich?" she asked.

"Sure."

Ronny opened the packages of lunchmeat and tortillas. "I suppose tortillas have gluten."

"You won't die. I doubt you're allergic to gluten anyway."

Ronny slapped two lunchmeat slices onto two tortillas, rolled them up and handed one to Cassie.

"We need to go to that grocery store," Cassie said. "We also need to find a place to hide that money."

"I'm thinking about it," Ronny said.

"We'll sleep in shifts."

"Sleep? Are you kidding? No, sir. I'm staying awake. I'm not going to take a chance on a thief catching me sleeping."

"Go to bed, Ronny. Get some rest. I'll take the first shift. Get into your pajamas and your winter coat and just go to bed. Tomorrow's going to be a busy day."

"I'm not taking my clothes off, no sir. If I have to run, I don't want to be naked."

CHAPTER 5

THE AROMA OF brewing coffee startled Cassie awake. Her cheek was resting on the primitive kitchen table. She sat upright, stiff-necked, and groggily scanned her surroundings. Through a squint she saw her sister standing at the kitchen counter pouring coffee into two thick mugs. She was wearing her winter coat, flannel pajama bottoms with pink flamingos, a pair of cowboy boots and her long thick hair in a loose knot on top of her head.

"Oh, my gosh, I fell asleep," Cassie said.

"Some night watchman *you* are," Ronny said, setting a mug of steaming coffee on the table in front of Cassie.

"Are those the cowboy boots one of the customers in the bar gave to you?" Cassie asked.

"Yep. Brought them to me all the way from Texas."

Cassie looked down at her own clothing. She was still wearing what she had traveled in—a sweater and jeans and her heavy winter coat. She rubbed her hands up and down her arms. "I'm freezing. This place doesn't even have heat."

"It did get cold last night. As warm as it was yesterday, it's hard to believe the temperature drop. We don't have a thermometer, so I don't know what the temperature is."

"It would be nice if we could build a fire in that fireplace."

"What would we use for wood. Look at the size of the thing. We could just scoot this kitchen table and chairs into it and have a bonfire in there."

"Wonder why they made it so big."

"As old as this place is, maybe they roasted a whole pig or something. It looks like a bunch of your fifth-grade students built it."

"Where did you put the money?"

"Under my pillow. I slept on it."

Cassie sipped the eye-opening brew and her eyes nearly crossed. Ronny made coffee with the same flamboyance she did everything else. "Oh, that hits the spot."

"Want some breakfast?" Ronny asked. "We've got lunchmeat on a tortilla and lunchmeat on a tortilla. I think they call that a burrito."

"Don't we have eggs?"

"But we have no butter or cooking oil."

"A lunchmeat burrito sounds great."

Ronny busied herself spreading mayonnaise on two tortillas and slapping a slice of lunchmeat onto each. She rolled up the sandwiches and handed one to Cassie.

"What do you think in the bright light of day?" Cassie asked and bit into her sandwich.

"About our inheritance?" Ronny took the chair opposite her. "Well, Little Sister, I feel like I've landed on another planet. You want to know what I *really* think?"

"I asked, didn't I? Go ahead. I'm ready for it."

"I think we're in deep shit. This place makes my crappy apartment back in Tonawilla look like a mansion. No way can we live here for a week, much less a year, even if the old man left us *fifty* thousand instead of twenty. Hell, we'll use it all up buying gasoline so we can look for civilization. If he wanted to give us something, why in the hell didn't he just sell all of this"—she made a sweeping gesture with her hand—"and give us the money?"

Cassie heaved a sigh. "You're right. We can't even benefit from selling the land ourselves. If we don't stay here a year and if we sell it before that, the ASPCA gets the money. How did he know we don't have families and a life in Tonawilla to keep us from uprooting and moving to Texas for a year?"

"Do you suppose he was keeping tabs on us without us knowing?"

Cassie had wondered about that herself, but she dismissed the thought before going deeper. "You mean spying on us?"

"I mean stalking."

Cassie rose to refill her coffee mug, then turned to her sister. "It doesn't matter now. We're here. You've signed, I've signed. Back in Tonawilla, we gave both our landlords notice and we packed and stored our stuff." She began to pace. "We've got to get organized and come up with a plan to make some money. I can keep teaching the rest of the school year by remote and I'll still be getting a paycheck. But it's only for four and a half months."

"They won't have summer school?"

"Not for fifth graders."

"And where does that leave me? I don't know how to do anything but bang on a cash register and mix drinks."

Cassie returned to her seat across from her sister. She tapped on the tabletop with her forefinger. "We have to figure out a way for you to get a paycheck. Maybe you could get a job at the grocery store like Mr. Atwater said."

"Minimum wage and probably part-time. I wouldn't make enough to make the twelve-mile drive."

"Maybe there's another town closer than Harlingen." Ronny's face wore a less-than-enthusiastic expression. "Ronny, look. We'll figure it out."

Ronny passed a flattened hand over her face. "See this face? Does it look like I'm figuring it out?"

"We have to think positive. Think how lucky we are."

"You know what? I am tired of your sunshiny attitude. My God, Cassie. You could be in a rainstorm standing in a mudpuddle and still think it was a pretty day."

"The return ticket is open, but I say we put it away for now. We can use it a year from now if we want to."

"Not go back, even to get our stuff?" Ronny clasped her head between both hands. "This is making me crazy. What about the things we need?"

"Ronny, our *stuff* doesn't amount to much. Everything we need is right here."

"Not really," Ronny snapped. "Look around. No washer or dryer. Half of our clothes were spread all over an asphalt parking lot and need to be washed.

No dishwasher or microwave. I doubt if there's a liquor store in *Lost* Tropicos and I think I'm going to need one." She threw a hand in the air. "I could rave on all day."

And she could, too, Cassie knew. She had reacted like Drama Queen Ronny, just as Cassie expected.

"What if I need new clothes?"

"Like what? You brought enough clothes to last a year, through all four seasons. I can't imagine what you're going to do with the two fancy cocktail dresses you said you brought, but whatever."

Ronny lifted her chin and sniffed. "I didn't know what to expect from this trip." Then she added, "But four seasons is right. We've been here less than twenty-four hours and we've had all four seasons already."

Cassie drew a deep breath. "Ronny, I'm tired. I'm just saying, let's give this a chance for now. Let's let the return tickets be our safety net. If the worse happens, we can always go home."

"Are we talking tomorrow?"

"A year, Ronny. A year." Cassie stood at attention and placed her right hand on her heart. "I swear on the state of New York if this doesn't work out, a year from now, we'll go back to Tonawilla and I won't even argue about it."

Ronny stood, too. "As long as we're talking about clothes, I'm going to get my suitcases and unpack. I can't believe I talked you into leaving them on the car all night after what Mr. Atwater said."

"You could have gone outside and gotten them. I didn't stop you. All I did was remind you of the snakes and varmints."

"After Atwater's speech. I don't know if I want to go outside in the daylight either, but here goes."

Ronny left through the front door. Cassie straightened the kitchen, checked out what she might find behind the cabinet doors, making a mental inventory. It looked as if they had enough pots and pans and—

Just then, Ronny strode back into the living room, loaded down with three suitcases. "It's orange."

"What's orange?"

"The whole damn place. That wall out front. The walls of the house. Everything is orange except those two palm trees by the fountain and the blue front door."

"That should make you happy. You wanted palm trees. Is it an ugly orange?"

"Nah. It's just orange. I'm going to unpack. Now I know why nobody stole our stuff. They couldn't figure out how to un-attach it from that little car. And after I unpack, I'm headed for the shower. I know we've got one. I saw it last night when I went to pee."

A minute later, Cassie heard a loud shriek. She quickstepped toward the bathroom, found Ronny standing on the toilet seat, blocked by the biggest cockroach she had ever seen, its antennae bobbing.

Cassie, too, shrieked and jumped back. "Oh, my gosh! What is it?"

"It looks like a friggin' man-eating cockroach. Find something to kill it with," Ronny begged, "like a baseball bat or something."

Cassie grabbed a can of hairspray from the counter

and gave the bug a blast of hairspray. It seemed to shudder but was otherwise unaffected.

"Wait a minute. I saw a broom in the kitchen. I'll be right back."

Cassie rushed to the kitchen and grabbed the broom. Back in the bathroom, she whacked at the giant roach but only stunned it. She got the broom behind it and swept it toward the bathroom door, through the kitchen and out the back door.

"You can get down now," she called to Ronny.

Ronny appeared in the kitchen, her fists planted on her hips. "I want to use that return ticket. I'm not living in a house with bugs the size of cats."

"Ronny, calm down. We'll find out how to get rid of them. As soon as we find out what they are."

"The water is a trickle," Ronny griped. "I don't know how I'm going to wash my hair. I'm going to need a bucket."

Cassie had been looking forward to a long, hot shower. "Oh, no. A shower is one of the necessities of life."

"The shower head is corroded. When it gets warmer, we need to tinker with it and see if we can make it work better." Ronny buttoned her coat. "I'm going out and see what the outside looks like in daylight. You should come with me."

"Okay, let me find better shoes."

Ronny left through the front door again while Cassie searched for a pair of socks and the hiking boots she had bought for a reason she no longer remembered and had rarely worn.

Within a minute the door flew open and banged the wall. Ronny stormed in. "Cassie! Cassie, come outside! There's a guy on a horse riding toward this place!"

On a jolt of panic, a rock dropped in Cassie's stomach. "Who is it?"

"Hopalong Cassidy? How the hell to I know?"

"You watch too many old movies, Ronny." With one boot on, one boot off, Cassie limped to the doorway and peered out.

Ronny came up behind her, looking over her shoulder. "Look at him. I mean, he is really riding. Galloping at full speed. Look at his hair, blowing in the wind. Do you suppose Indians are chasing him? What do we do? Should we call nine-one-one?"

"Settle down, Dances with Wolves. I don't think cowboys have been chased by Indians in a very long time. Even in Texas. If we were back home, what would we do?"

"If a cowboy rode up on horseback? Hah. I'd call Bellevue."

"No. We'd go outside and see what he wants, which is exactly what I intend to do."

Cassie limped outside into the sunlight. Ronny followed.

The man on horseback had slowed his horse to a trot and was now only a few yards away. Cassie could see he was wearing a short denim jacket over a white shirt and jeans. Even from a distance, she could also see that his body was perfectly built.

"Oh. My. Gosh. Where did he come from?"

"Fantasy Island," Ronny mumbled quietly.

The nearer he came the better Cassie could see his thighs pressed hard against the horse's sides. Muscular arms showed even through his jacket as he pulled on the reigns. Mirrored aviator sunglasses perched beneath a gray cowboy hat. Fantasy was right. What real person went around looking like that? And dressing like that?

A trigger tripped inside Cassie. It wasn't fear exactly, but it was something just as profound.

He stopped his horse a few feet away and dismounted. He lifted off his hat and sunglasses. "Mornin', ladies."

"Hey," Ronny said, lifting two fingers.

Oh, my gosh. His eyes are brown, dark and mysterious. "Goo—good morning," Cassie managed, totally distracted by his square jaw and his jaw-length hair. It was black and shiny, full of body, waves and bounce, the kind any woman would envy. She thought cowboys wore short, clipped hair, but his was wild and free. She suddenly thought about running her fingers through it and—

Just then, Ronny said. "Are you a real cowboy?"

Chuckling, the visitor re-set his hat. "I like to think I am, but it's a stretch." He showered them with a bone-melting smile. "The Jennings sisters, I presume. I hope I didn't startle you. My name's Boudreaux McKenzie Buckalew, but my friends call me Bo."

"I'll just bet they do," Ronny said dryly.

Cassie gripped the door facing behind her. Her mouth had gone dry. "Hello" was all she could utter when she really wanted to say, *Would you like to take your clothes off?*

She was shocked at herself. She'd never in her life experienced something so strong as the sensations coursing through her. Certainly, she had never felt anything like it with Frank.

"I'm Ronny Jennings and this is my sister Cassie. We just got here last night. From New York."

She looked to Cassie as if for confirmation, but Cassie was having trouble keeping her wits about her. "New York. Yes, last night, New York, the state."

The cowboy smiled, showing perfect teeth. "Pax told me you were coming. I meant to be here when you arrived, but I got sidetracked by an ornery bull."

"You know Mr. Atwater? He didn't mention you," Ronny said.

"It must have slipped his mind. Your daddy was a friend of mine. He appointed me to keep an eye on your place until you got here. I've also been seeing to the four cows he left you."

"We haven't seen the cows yet," Cassie said. "Where are they?"

"This morning, they were on the south end of the pasture grazing. There's a windmill down there and the water tank's full, so they're okay. I put out some hay."

To Cassie, he might as well have been speaking Greek. She had seen pictures of a windmill before, but she had no idea what it had to with a water tank.

"Your daddy loved those ol' cows," the visitor went on. "He rescued them from slaughter."

"Oh, I see," Cassie said, though she didn't see at all. In fact, she had been blinded by the sight of Bo Buckalew.

"He hoped you'd get to love them, too. They're gentle as lambs. Tomorrow, I can come over with my mule and take you out to where they're grazing and you can meet them."

"You expect us to ride a mule?" Ronny said, incredulous. "Is that different from riding a horse?"

Bo chuckled. "A mule is a four-wheeled vehicle, sort of like a golf cart, but tougher."

"This whole thing is a bit much for us to take in," Ronny said. "We lived in a small town but small town or not, New York is New York, right?"

"True. I've been to the city a couple of times. It's a...well, it's a unique place. I live on the next place over, by the way."

"The next place? Is that a trailer park? A town?" Cassie asked.

"No, ma'am. Neither one. I'm your neighbor. My land butts up against yours."

Cassie fought back tears. She was saying stupid things and making a fool of herself in front of this handsome stranger, but she couldn't seem to control her tongue. She had never been where she couldn't carry on a conversation. Taking a deep breath she said, "Ronny, I'm going inside. My foot is freezing. You two sort it out about the cows." She turned and limped back through the doorway.

Inside the house, she stood at the door she had left open a few inches, peeking out.

Bo was looking at Ronny, his brow tented with a frown. "Is she alright?"

"She's fine. Jet lag, probably. Would you like to come inside?"

Cassie willed her thoughts to her sister. *Ronny! No, no, no!*

"Don't have time. I've got to get to Harlingen. Got some errands to run and got to pick up a few things.

I go up there about once a week. I usually bring back stuff if people need it. You girls need anything?"

"We need a lot of things," Ronny said. "Mostly food and water and another bed. A washer and dryer would be nice. We also need to go to a bank. You wouldn't let us ride with you, would you?"

Cassie clamped her teeth. *Eek! No, Ronny!*

"Sure. Why not?" Bo regathered his reins, stepped up into the stirrup and swung onto his saddle.

Cassie's knees went weak.

"I'll be back in a couple of hours to pick you up in my truck."

Ronny gave a thumbs up. Bo touched the brim of his hat with two fingers and loped away.

Cassie grabbed a shirt and began wiping a table she had already wiped.

Ronny came back in and slammed the front door. "Is that a trailer park?" she mocked. "A trailer park, for chrissakes. New York, last night, New York, the state." Ronny cackled. "Hell, Cassie, I thought you were having a stroke or some out-of-body experience."

Cassie sank to a chair at the table. "Just drop it. That was embarrassing. I don't understand what happened. It was like I've never seen a cowboy before."

Refilling her mug with coffee, Ronnie gave her a look "When did you ever see a cowboy?"

"In movies. You know, theaters and TV."

"Well, Sister, I don't know a lot about cowboys, but I get a taste of a few of them now and then in the bar. They flirt and tease and make you think you're a princess. They call you "darlin'" and "sugar" and say yes, ma'am and no ma'am. They sweep off their big hats and open doors for you. That whole chivalry routine works. It just does." She heaved a sigh. "Yep, they can sure be intoxicating, but they're snakes. Some of them are more dangerous than a snake. You have to watch out for them."

"Why haven't you ever taken up with one of them?"

"Who says I haven't?"

"You mean you've slept with one of them? I thought you refused to go out with men you met at work."

"I do. Most of the time."

"You've never said anything."

Ronny gave a little gasp. "I don't tell you every private moment of my life."

Now Cassie was annoyed at her sister keeping secrets. "What are cowboys doing in Tonawilla anyway?" she griped. "Dairy cows are the only cows we have."

"Mostly driving truck. Long-haulers passing through. The Do-Drop-In Motel in Tonawilla has a place to park their trucks and cheap rooms to lay over in before they turn around and head back west." Ronny gestured with an upward motion of one hand. "Get up and get your ass in gear. Bo will be back to pick us up in a couple of hours."

"I can't believe you asked him to take us to Harlingen. Mr. Atwater said we have a pickup in the barn and it runs."

"That might be a matter in interpretation. We don't know if we can drive it. And we don't know if it's even insured. Today we've got a ride to Harlingen using someone else's gas."

Cassie got to her feet and picked up her suitcase

Ronny had brought in, but she stopped and asked her sister, "If he was friends with our father, do you suppose he knows about the money? I think it's illegal for Mr. Atwater to have told him, but—"

"Maybe the old man told him. Or maybe he doesn't know. Whatever. We just need to put it in the bank. It's making me nervous. I'm already tired of sleeping on my satchel."

"Right. We can open a savings account maybe. Or a checking account. Maybe I'll have worked up an immunity to that cowboy before he comes back."

CHAPTER 6

TEXAS RANGER BO Buckalew unsaddled his horse and lifted the saddle onto a saddle tree in his barn's tack room. Riding Dusty to and from the Jennings place had been a steady workout for the horse, so he needed cooling down. Bo grasped his halter and walked him around the corral and on out into the pasture.

After their walk, Bo brushed him, then wiped down his gear and put the various parts in their respective places. He hung his saddle pad over the edge of the stall to dry completely.

He should have been back to the Jennings place half an hour ago, but any cowboy worth his salt took care of his horse before anything else.

All the while he was grooming Dusty, he thought of the Jennings sisters. They seemed like nice women. Both were more attractive than he had imagined. In some ways, the tall one resembled their father.

Bo knew only a little about them. John Jennings had talked about them from time to time, but Bo never dreamed they would actually make the trip to Texas and take up a claim on the land. He would have bet that two women from New York would have turned their backs on the dumb requirement to inherit, yet here they were. Did they know what a devious character their father had been?

That question took his thoughts to John Jennings. Bo had been operating undercover, building a relationship with him for more than a year. Among the many things he had learned about Jennings was the fact that the dude lived on the edge. He was frequently back and forth across the border and no doubt had some dangerous acquaintances and he had an unknown source of income.

Bo had worried about everything from bandits to one of the cartels taking Jennings out prematurely. Even drunk driving because John had liked his Jack Daniel's. Bo hadn't even considered COVID.

Jennings had come down with a chest cold, was hospitalized with pneumonia in Harlingen, followed by his being moved to ICU. Despite being a relatively young man, age fifty-five, within two weeks of entering the hospital he was gone. Hours of meticulous information gathering wiped out.

Bo sighed. All he could do now was take what he had already learned, try to discern if the daughters had anything to contribute and hope for an outcome that would send him home to Marfa in West Texas. He had lived in South Texas long enough.

"See ya later, buddy," Bo told Dusty and walked back to his house.

Cassie's frustration knew no bounds. She had shivered through a shower, such as it was. Now, wearing her winter coat over jeans and a sweater, she flitted from room to room, her make-up mirror cord in hand. She had tried every plug-in in the house. Apparently, only one person could plug something extra into overloaded electrical circuits and Ronny already had her hair dryer plugged in.

"Let me know when you're finished," she called to her sister.

Ronny came out of the bathroom, hairbrush in one hand, dryer in the other. Ronny's hair was thick and shiny and beautiful, even with red and green streaks, but it took a lot of time and pampering.

"Why are you so worried about your makeup?" she asked. "You've already been seen by the good-looking stranger."

Busted! Cassie felt her cheeks turning warm. "I just so happen to care about my appearance when meeting strangers is all."

"Oh yeah? Since when? I've never seen you wear anything but a little foundation and some blush, no matter who you were meeting. I've wanted to do your makeup for years. Come sit down and let me work on you."

Pull it together, Cassie.

"No! You'd—well…maybe. But I just want a touch-up before what's-his-name comes back," Cassie added quickly. "I don't need to be runway ready." She pressed a finger against her cheek. "I wonder if he has other means of transportation than his horse. That could present a problem."

Ronny had put down her brush and the hair dryer.

She stood behind one chair, a dozen little brushes and tubes in one hand. "He's coming back in a pickup, goofball. Stop trying to change the subject. I have never, I repeat *never*, seen this side of you. I kind of like you rattled and second guessing yourself....Take a seat, Little Sister."

Cassie dropped to the chair facing her sister. If Ronny thought she had acted strangely, what might the cowboy have thought?

"It's not like he's the first man I've ever met."

"But he's the first cowboy."

Just as Ronny had swiped a brush of color to Cassie's right cheek, carefully highlighting the hollow in her cheek to create a high cheekbone, the growl and clatter of a vehicle approaching rattled dishes in the cabinets.

"Oh, my gosh, what is that noise?" Cassie asked.

Ronny put down a makeup brush, walked over and opened the front door. The engine clatter became deafening.

The noise subsided and Bo Buckalew walked into the house. "Hey, sorry I'm a little late. Y'all ready to go?"

"We're ready." Ronny scooped up her satchel and grabbed the list she had been making. The list that had started with one or two items had grown considerably.

"But wait," Cassie said. "You didn't finish me."

But Ronny was already out the door and the cowboy was standing in the doorway motioning to her, Cassie. "Let's get going. We're burning daylight."

Cassie got to her feet and rushed out the door.

The pickup was a massive white vehicle of some

sort with four doors. Agile as a monkey, Ronny opened the back door and sprang onto the backseat with little effort.

Oh, no, Cassie thought. That meant she would have to ride upfront. The role of talking would fall to her and she could already feel her throat going dry. Bo opened the front door on the passenger side, then rounded the pickup's frontend and climbed behind the steering wheel.

Cassie took one look at the floorboard and knew she was in trouble. It was at least three feet off the ground.

"Need a hand?" Bo asked.

If my older sister can do it, I can do it. "Uh, no. I've got it."

Purse in hand, trying to emulate her sister's Olympic mount, Cassie bent her knees and sprang, landed flat on her face on the front passenger seat, floundering like some damn fish out of water. If only her head would hit something and render her unconscious.

Bo offered his hand. Grunting, she grasped it, but with her legs flailing behind her, she couldn't get traction.

"Just a minute," Bo said, releasing her hand and dismounting. Then, he was behind her. "Ma'am, I need you to stop kicking so I can help you."

Cassie went stiff and still, her legs like planks sticking out of the passenger side. Thank God she wasn't wearing a dress. She could hear Ronny trying not to laugh, the snickering worse than guffaws.

She felt a firm grip on her ankles, her knees bending as this stranger moved her into a sitting position, then fastened her seat belt. No man except Frank had ever touched her body. Mortified was the only word Cassie could think of that wasn't a cuss word. Totally mortified.

"I'm so sorry," she said, on the verge of tears.

"Don't worry. You're not the first tiny woman who's had trouble with my truck."

And just exactly how many tiny women would that be? A dark emotion she could only label jealousy oozed through her. Of course, a man with his looks had a bevy of women.

Stop it, Cassie! Why do you care? You don't even know him and you don't need him anyway. After all, you've got Frank.

"These trucks were built this way for a reason and getting in was not the reason," Bo added with a killer smile. He returned to his place behind the steering wheel and looked at her across the console. "Everything okay now?"

"Fine," she answered, tight jawed.

A half smirk sneaked across is mouth. Was he trying not to laugh?

"Okay, then." He pressed the start button and the loud clatter started up again.

"It certainly is noisy, isn't it?"

"It's a diesel engine."

Cassie didn't know a diesel engine from any other kind. Out of words, she pulled down the visor and opened the panel covering the mirror and almost groaned aloud. She might not be the first woman to have trouble getting into his pickup, but she knew for sure she was the first to have one cheek made up to cover girl perfection while the other was white as a baby's bottom. She looked like a clown. No wonder he had held back a laugh.

Damn, you, Ronny!

This embarrassment was her sister's fault. Cassie slapped the panel closed over the mirror, hiding her reflection.

She had to remedy her situation. She pawed and dug inside her purse. As if he had read her mind, Bo said, "I keep some wet wipes in the console. Help yourself."

"Oh, thank you."

She opened the console and plucked a couple of the damp wipes out of their container, wiped away the foundation and blush Ronny had put on her face. Now her face was one color again—red.

"Hey," Bo said, "I didn't notice."

Liar, liar, pants on fire. "Yes, you did. I saw you smirk. For your information, Ronny was in the middle of making up my face when you showed up."

Flipping the sun visor mirror back in position she arranged her shirt beneath the confines of the seat beat and looked straight ahead.

"So, Bo," Ronny said from the backseat, "your wife isn't mad about your taking us to Harlingen with you, is she?"

Cassie rolled her eyes. Could Ronny be more obvious? Still, she felt a spike of adrenaline as she waited for his answer.

"Don't have a wife," Bo said.

Cassie felt Ronny's foot under her seat and pushing up. At the same time, she breathed a sigh of relief.

"Tell me about yourselves," Bo said. "Your daddy

talked a little bit about you, but he didn't tell me how pretty y'all are."

Bo's flattery couldn't overcome the bitterness Cassie felt toward the father she knew in name only. "How would he know anything about us? He shouldn't even be talking about us. Ronny and I were babies when he left us."

"World's worst excuse for a father," Ronny put in from the backseat.

Bo cleared his throat, his eyes on the road ahead. Minutes of silence passed.

Ronny leaned forward, her head between Cassie and Bo. "This is our first trip to Texas. Cassie teaches school. I marry losers. First, I married a mechanic. He taught me how to work on cars. Then I followed up with a lawyer. He taught me that lawyers are snakes who cheat on their wives. My last husband was a builder. He taught me how to build a house. Bet our dad didn't tell you all that. He probably didn't even know it."

"Uh, no ma'am. He didn't tell me."

Ronny went on giving a colorful description of the life she and her sister had, making it sound much more interesting than it actually was.

"You said you've been to New York City," Cassie said. "Did you hate it?"

"Yeah," Ronny said. "I can't see you taking a bite out of the Big Apple."

"Actually, I didn't mind it. I took a trip with my nephew to West Point. We stayed in the city for a couple of days. It's not somewhere I'd want to live forever, but for a visit, it was interesting."

"How so?" Cassie asked.

"Well, I'd been warned, and even thought so myself, that everyone in New York City would be rude and in too big of a hurry to slow down and talk to you, but the people I ran into were nice. Helpful even."

"Were you wearing your cowboy suit?" Ronny asked. "I hate to make you think New Yorkers aren't nice, but it was because you're a cowboy."

"She's right," Cassie said. "Some people fall all to pieces at the sight of a real live cowboy."

"What do you do for a living, Bo?" Ronny asked. "I know being caretaker of John Jennings' vast estate can't pay that much."

"It doesn't pay anything, ma'am. When he got sick, I offered to help him out. After he ended up in ICU and quarantined, there wasn't a chance to discuss much with him. Then he passed so fast.... But helping out a neighbor. That's what friends are for, right?"

"I wouldn't know," Ronny said. "The only friend I've ever had slept with my husband. That was Husband Number Two."

Inside, Cassie winced. She worried about hearing her sister make comments to a stranger that were so personal. Ronny was such a motor mouth.

Cassie thought about the money they now had. She cleared her throat that was drying more by the minute, "Are there places to shop in Harlingen? I don't remember seeing many stores when we were there."

"Yes ma'am, there's a Walmart and a Target. If you want something more upscale there's a mall. They'll have fancy stuff you might want."

"A mall?" Ronny asked, excited. "There's a mall?"

"Yes ma'am," Bo replied, eyes glued on a road with no sign of traffic in either direction.

Robby giggled. "I might be able to last a year after all."

"Can I ask you something?" Cassie said. "This 'yes ma'am', 'no ma'am', 'thank you ma'am', what's that all about?"

"Ma'am?"

"You did it again. Why? We aren't that old."

Bo chuckled. "Ma'am, Texas was a part of the Confederacy and after the War of Northern Aggression, a lot of people migrated here from the southern states and—"

"The War of Northern Aggression?" Cassie asked. "Are you talking about the Civil War?"

"Yes, ma'am."

"The War of Northern Aggression," Ronny repeated and laughed. "Hah, I like that."

"Anyway," Bo continued, "some of the old southern customs still hang on. My mama's family came from Alabama and she insisted on it. It has nothing to do with age. It's meant to show respect. If I didn't say it, I'd be telling the world I wasn't raised right and she would've been embarrassed. She also would've tanned my hide."

"I assume that means spanking. You don't have to keep it up for us," Cassie said. "And I don't believe in hitting children."

"Don't pay any attention to her," Ronny said. "She teaches ten-year-olds. I don't mind hearing you say ma'am. I think it's sort of cute and sexy, especially when you add that darling drawl."

A flush of pink showed through on Bo's tanned

face, making him even better looking than he already was.

Cassie shot Ronny a wilting glare. "I think it's sexy too," she blurted out, causing his blush to amplify. "I mean, you know, respect itself is sexy and kids should learn that. Not that they should learn to be sexy, but they should be taught to be polite. Because believe me, there is nothing sexy about being rude. I mean, if you're going to have a drawl, you need to make it sexy."

"Well, ma'am, I didn't know I had a drawl."

Cassie closed her eyes and drew a breath through her nose. She was blabbing like an idiot. She had just used the word sexy half a dozen times and insulted his speech.

Maybe Ronny was right. They should return to New York because aliens had taken over her mind and body and turned her into one big fool who probably needed to have her hide tanned.

CHAPTER 7

AFTER SEVERAL HOURS, most of the tasks on
Ronny's list had been checked off. They had
opened a checking account and a savings account.
They had bought cleaning supplies, a bed, a mattress
and bedding for the second bedroom and a week's
worth of groceries. Ronny had nagged Cassie into
buying a pair of cowboy boots.

As they left Harlingen, Bo said, "I gotta hand it
to you girls. You got a whole lot more done than I
thought you would. Good thing my truck's bed has
a cover."

"We did do good," Ronny said. "We needed
everything from bed pillows to extension cords and
beyond."

They hadn't eaten all day. For a long time, hunger
pangs had gnawed at Cassie's stomach. "Am I the only
one hungry? Our breakfast of coffee and lunchmeat
on a tortilla was a long time ago. Bo, if you'd be
willing to stop for something to eat, we'll be happy
to buy your dinner."

"No need for that. I'll show you some Texas

hospitality. I'll take you to get the best supper you've ever had."

He pulled off the highway, drove a short distance on a dirt road and stopped in front of a, a, well…a shack. Behind it, inside a large, fenced area where several cows stood lazily chewing hay. When he opened the pickup door, an obnoxious odor filled the air around them.

"*Phew*," Ronny said. "If this is a place to eat, I hope that odor isn't coming from the kitchen."

Cassie pinched off her nostrils with her left hand while she fanned the air with the right. "I just lost my appetite. It smells like…well, it smells like—"

"Cow manure." Bo said on a chuckle. "This is a feed lot. Y'all wait just a minute. I'll bring you supper."

He stepped out of the pickup and disappeared into the ramshackle building.

Ronny leaned forward. "Is he kidding? What's a feed lot? They serve food? This whole trip feels like I've landed in The Twilight Zone. Is someone filming this?"

"I know what you mean," Cassie said, frowning and chewing on her thumbnail.

"Is supper the same thing as dinner? Am I going to have to learn a new language down here?"

"In the South, I think supper and dinner are the same thing. From the looks of things, if you need to learn a new language, it should be Spanish."

After they sat in silence for a few minutes, Ronny said, "You know something? He's a good-looking man. If you weren't all gaga over him, I'd make a run at him myself."

Making a little gasp, Cassie turned in her seat to

look at her sister, "Me, gaga? I am not gaga over him. I think he's cute, but—"

Ronny opened her palms. "Puppies are cute, Sister. Babies are cute. That man is hot. Hot as Texas."

"I think he's very nice and patient is what I was going to say. Why would a man who hardly knows us take us around and wait while we shop and even help us find things? Frank would be complaining and having a fit."

Ronny flopped a limp hand. "Forget Frank Kowalski and his elevator shoes."

Cassie's jaw clenched. Ronny always made fun of Frank's height. Okay, so barefooted he was no taller than Cassie. So what?

Then Ronny giggled mischieviously. "Maybe Bo's into you too. Have you thought of that?"

"Don't you dare tease me in front of him. It's all I can do to even speak to him. I'm still mad at you over leaving me with a half-made-up face."

"May I say, Dear Sister, it's about time you looked at some guy besides that fool, Frank. I promise to be good. I wouldn't jeopardize this for the world. My little Cassie and a hunky cowboy. Who would have ever thought?"

Bo returned with Styrofoam cups in both hands. "I didn't think to ask. Hope Cokes are okay."

Ronnie reached for the tall drink. "Thanks. Right now, I'd take a shot of vinegar. We haven't even had a drink of water all day." She took a long pull on her straw and made a scowly face. "*Blech!* This isn't Coke."

"Dr. Pepper," Bo said and strode back into the building.

"What's wrong with these people?" Ronny said. "They don't know the difference between Coke and Dr. Pepper?"

"They don't seem to. You heard the conversation I had with that girl back at Taco Fiesta."

"Don't remind me. I'm trying to forget Taco Fiesta and their damn parking lot. I'm still trying to figure out where we're going to wash our clothes that were spread all over the asphalt."

Bo came back again with a huge aromatic sack. "Bet you girls have never had real Texas barbecue."

Cassie reached for the sack and peeked inside. "No, we haven't."

"There's a shady spot right up this road a little ways. There's a concrete table and bench seats. We'll stop and have a picnic."

Indeed, the table was shaded by several tall palm trees. The temperature had climbed to a pleasant 85-degrees. "Days like this are why snowbirds come here," Bo said, taking plastic spoons and forks out of the sack, followed by three large paper trays with thick burgers and French fries.

"Snowbirds come here?" Cassie asked, looking at her burger with sliced meat protruding all the way around.

"Yep. Every winter. Some come all the way from Canada. They do a lot for the local economy."

"I thought snowbirds only went to Florida." Ronny lifted the top off her burger and stared at the inside. "What is this? It doesn't look like bacon. You know what? I guess I can eat the French fries."

"Come on. Give it a try," Bo said. "It's sliced brisket.

I've never met anybody who doesn't like barbecued brisket."

Cassie was still studying her sandwich. "This almost looks like a hamburger, but it isn't. What is brisket?"

"Brisket is a cut of beef. Tough if it isn't cooked right. Real good barbecued. They used to make hamburger out of it, but now, it's like steak."

"Oh, yeah," Ronny said. "I've heard of it. A few customers where I work at home talk about it. We don't have it in Tonawilla."

Bo opened three Styrofoam cups of beans, three more of Cole slaw, still two others of slices of peppers and pickles. Finally, a cup of something red with a tangy aroma. "This is barbecue sauce. The smoked meat is plenty good all by itself, but a little sauce makes it larruppin'."

Cassie couldn't hold back a giggle and hid her mouth behind her hand.

He gave her a look. "What?"

"It's just that I love hearing you talk."

He blushed again. He lifted off the top of his burger and spooned the red sauce over the meat sandwich. "Add some jalapeno slices and dig in. Better than a prime rib dinner, in my opinion."

"I've never had beans like this before," Cassie said.

"Pinto beans. *Frijoles,* the Mexicans call them. If you grew up in Texas, especially rural Texas, you grew up eating pinto beans."

"Hunh," Ronny said. "I just always thought beans were beans."

Sure enough, the food was delicious. They ate the whole thing, all the while, talking and laughing at

Bo's drawl and Ronny's smart aleck commentary.

Soon they were on the road again. The sun hung low in the sky, creating layers of gold and pink. "Bet you've never seen a sunset as pretty as this," Bo said.

"I don't think we have," Cassie replied, relaxed and feeling better about their trip to Texas. "Bo, we appreciate all you've done for us today. And we appreciate your buying us dinner. I'm uncomfortable asking for another favor, but—"

"Shoot," Bo replied.

"We have to have the rental car back to the airport by next Tuesday, but it would cost us less if we could get it back sooner. I was wondering—"

"No problem. I can follow you back to the airport. But I forgot to mention the truck your dad left you. What do you think of it?"

"Mr. Atwater told us about it, but we haven't yet had the chance to look at it."

"It runs like a top. Purrs right along."

"That's what Mr. Atwater said." Cassie slid her hand over the tan leather upholstery on the arm of her chair. There were probably plenty of people in Tonawilla who had pickups with leather upholstery, but she didn't know them. "Your pickup is so nice. Is the one we've inherited like yours?"

"Not exactly. We'll take a look at it when we get back to Los Tropoicos. I guess you can say we're saving it for last."

The words "saving it for last" gave Cassie a bad feeling. "Okay, now you're scaring me. What's wrong with it?"

"It's in perfect running condition."

"You keep saying that," Ronny popped off from

the backseat. "Why do I feel like there's a *but* at the end of that sentence?"

Twilight had descended by the time they reached the little orange house.

All three grabbed packages and bags and carried them indoors. They carried the new mattress and bed into the bedroom.

The home's interior was surprisingly cool. "Wow, it's cool in here," Cassie said.

"That's the way it is in these old adobe structures," Bo replied. "The old Spaniards figured out a way to live with the heat. It'll take a couple of days for it to warm up after the cold snap."

"Is the cold snap over?"

"Mostly. Cold weather never lasts more than a couple of days."

"Time to see this mode of transportation we'll have for a year," Cassie said. "Bo, can you show us."

"Can do. It's parked in the barn. Nobody has been back there for a while and the grass has grown up. This time of day, it'll be safer if I drive you back there."

Ronny stopped in her tracks. "Wait a minute. You're talking about snakes. What kind of snakes?"

"Rattlesnakes mostly. We've got other snakes, but the rattlers are the ones you need to look out for."

"Those are the ones that'll kill you," Ronny said. "Sister, I need to inspect the bathroom. I'm relying on you to tell me how good or bad our new wheels are." She emphasized "new wheels" with air quotes.

Cassie was as fearful of snakes as Ronny, but she rode with Bo back to the wooden barn. He stopped in front of double doors. "Is it okay to get out?" she asked.

"My truck makes enough noise and causes enough commotion anything that's hiding in the grass has headed for the hills. You're wearing boots. You see, cowboy boots are for more than just looking pretty. They also protect your feet and legs."

Cassie opened her door and cautiously stepped down. "Are you sure?"

"It's no problem, but when you come back here, you should carry a stick or something. Barns are ideal places for varmints to hang out. My yard man comes in a couple of days. I'll ask him to come over and mow this grass for you. Time sneaked up on me or I would have already had it done."

He dug a key from his jeans' pocket and unlocked the double doors, rolled them aside and walked into the barn. Lights came on inside and outside the barn.

Parked to the right of a stack of hay bales was an old metallic blue pickup. Cassie couldn't guess its age.

She was the first to admit she was no expert on pickups, had never ridden in one more than a few times. What she was looking at now was like nothing she had ever seen or read about. "What is that?" she asked, feeling her eyes bug.

"Fifty-seven Chevy. A classic. A lot of car collectors would love to have it. Your dad made sure it was kept up, regular oil changes and the like. I'll back it out so you can see it better."

He returned to the barn's interior and scooted into

the pickup. Suddenly loud trumpets and guitars from inside the barn splintered the nighttime silence. Bo backed the pickup out and parked it in the outdoor spotlight, the engine idling, the music blaring.

He stepped out of the pickup and came back to where she stood. "There it is," he yelled. "What do you think?"

The vehicle was just as Bo had described—an antique pickup. Classic? Collectible? Cassie didn't know. But it didn't matter. On top of the cab stood a large image—a taco at least five feet long and three feet high. The taco looked incredibly like the real thing—tan shell, green lettuce and red tomatoes.

"Well, it's, uh…colorful," Cassie shouted to be heard over the music. "I don't understand it, but I think I love it. My kids back in New York would call it *dope.*"

"I don't know if you'd want to do that," Bo yelled. "Dope is something we say very carefully in these parts."

Suddenly, Ronny rushed out of the house's back door, broom in hand. "*Jesus, Joseph and Mary!* What is going on?"

"What's that music it's playing?" Cassie asked Bo.

"Around here, you hear it a lot. It's mariachi music. That song is *El Rancho Grande.*"

"Oh, my gosh. It's a good thing we don't have any neighbors," Cassie said.

"Yeah," Ronny said. "They'd be calling the cops about the noise."

"It grows on you," Bo said. "Y'all can drive a stick, can't you?"

"Drive a stick?" Cassie parroted. "Is that another expression used here?"

"It's the transmission. A way to shift gears. You know, reverse, park, neutral? This pickup has four-on-the floor. You don't see it in cars built nowadays."

"The cars I've always driven didn't require anything on the floor but your purse," Cassie shouted.

The music continued to boom.

"Well ma'am, I'll be happy to teach you to drive it. Let me turn that music off so we can talk," Bo yelled back. He slid back into the pickup, drove it into the barn and glorious nighttime silence ensued.

With a beaming expression, Cassie turned to her sister. "It's a fifty-seven Chevy. It has a stick in the floor. And Bo's going to teach me how to drive it. You want to learn too?"

"Ahhh, no thanks, Trying to learn to drive a pickup with four-in-the floor is one of the reasons my first marriage ended. Besides, somehow, it seems more fitting for an elementary school teacher. That music could warn kids for miles around that you're on your way."

Ronny turned to Bo. "Somebody really drove this?"

"Your dad drove it. The original owner drove it, too."

"Is he the one who had this, uh...uh, statue welded on?"

"Yup. The original owner was from Mexico. He used the truck for his livelihood."

"Which was?" Cassie asked warily.

"He sold tacos and tamales. Some people thought he also sold illegal drugs. He had the taco image made by some guy in Harlingen. It's sort of like a disguise.

He's also the one who had the outstanding radio and speaker system installed. Even if people couldn't see him coming, they could hear him."

"If that, uh, statue is welded, does that mean the thing can't be removed?" Cassie asked.

Bo's attention came back to Cassie. "It's made of steel. I'm sure you could get somebody to cut it off, but it'd cost you a pretty penny and I don't know what it would do to the top of your truck. Your dad liked it."

Ronny faked a gagging attack. "*Gah!* It's awful."

"Maybe we could sell it to one of those collectors." Cassie said.

"Maybe," Bo replied. "But don't forget. It's like the rest of the property. If you don't hang on to it for a year, it and everything with it goes down the road and the money goes to ASPCA. Your dad loved animals."

"What a bastard," Ronny growled, her lips twisted in a horseshoe scowl. "He might've loved animals, but he sure didn't think much of his kids."

"I wouldn't say that's true," Bo said. "He left you everything he had."

"You said you were friends with him. Why would he leave us his stuff along with a demand to live in it and with it, whether we want to or not? Is it some kind of sick joke?"

"He loved living here. Guess he wanted you to have affection for it, too. But I know from personal experience, you have to stay here a while to learn to love it. He knew it would take some adjusting."

Cassie heaved a huge sigh. "We have to have transportation and we can't afford to buy a car. What could driving a truck decorated with a giant taco hurt? We can pretend it isn't there and we can just turn off the music."

"Well…that isn't exactly true," Bo said. "It's wired in. If you turn on the ignition, the music comes on and you can't shut it off unless you kill the engine. Period."

At a loss for words, Cassie stared up at him for a few empty seconds.

Ronny filled the void. "*Jee-zus Christ!* We're going to drive around in a truck playing music and with a taco on top, dispensing drugs like some damn ice cream truck?"

Bo's shoulders lifted in a shrug. "Well, you wouldn't be selling drugs, I presume."

Cassie beamed her gaze on her sister. "Or, Ronny, since you need an income, maybe you could learn to make tacos and tamales."

Ronny stared down at her. "*Hah!* I can't boil water. Of all the things I might like to learn, making and selling tacos and tamales is not one of them."

"You learned how to make pizza and tacos in Duffy's Tavern," Cassie argued. "You can make a mean margarita. You could add margaritas to the menu."

On a groan, Ronny shook her head and pressed her fingertips against her temples. "I knew I should've been going to mass and praying. We're being punished. Someone, anyone, please wake me from this nightmare."

"It could be worse," Cassie said. "If he needed to drive around in a taco and tamales truck to advertise himself, what if he had been a gynecologist or a male fertility specialist?"

Bo broke into laughter. "You girls are funny. Let's

get back into the house and put that bed together so
y'all will have a place to sleep tonight."

CHAPTER 8

AS THEY PUT together the bed, Ronny grumbled, "Too bad those old Spaniards didn't figure out the plumbing. It's shot."

"Oh?" Bo asked.

"There's barely enough water pressure to rinse your hair. The shower head is so corroded I'm surprised water comes out at all. And the kitchen faucet makes a singing noise. Speaking of water, where does our water come from?"

"From a well," Bo answered.

"A hole in the ground?" Ronny gasped. "My God, we're drinking that water!"

"I have a well myself and I like it. Los Tropicos has no municipal water system and even if it did, it wouldn't come all the way out here. Don't tell me people in rural New York don't have water wells."

"My old boss lives on five acres and he has a well."

"I'm sorry we're so stupid," Cassie said. "It's just that we've always lived in town and truthfully, I never thought about where the water came from. Ronny's just stressed out. She wasn't prepared for this experience and I'm guess I'm not either."

"There's more than that," Ronny griped. "The toilet needs a new seal and while it's removed it should be replaced with one that's a little taller. I feel like I'm falling through the floor when I sit down. We need a plumber."

"You sound like you know what you want," Bo said.

"My third husband was a builder. Sometimes, when we were speaking to each other, I helped him."

"I apologize, but I can't do any of that kind of work. However, I've got a friend who can. Is it okay if I have him call you?"

"Does he work cheap?"

"He'll work with you and he'll be fair."

"Guess that'll have to do for starters. What's his name?"

"Tex. Tex Barton."

On a sardonic laugh, Ronny turned to Cassie, "See? All the men around her are either cowboys or named for the state. Or both."

Before leaving, Bo arranged to return the next day and follow Cassie to the airport to return the rental car. His original intent had been to spend as much time as possible with the New York sisters, pumping for information, and he had dreaded it. Now, if it meant more time around Cassie, he found himself looking forward to it.

Driving away, he pressed his supervisor's saved number on his cell phone. After a couple of burrs, he was connected. "Hey, Pete, this is Bo. I got inside the house. The place looks just like it did when Jennings lived there. The fireplace is still there…."

A pause while Bo listened. "Uh-huh, it's pretty crude. Looks like it was slapped together by amateurs. Jennings might have even done it himself. I'm sure Atwater told these two women not to use it…. Uh-huh….Uh-huh. The women didn't bring anything new or unusual. I don't think they know anything about what their dad did…."

Another pause. "Yep. They've got to live there a year. They want to do some remodeling. Minor stuff. I know a local man who can do the work and I won't have to disclose anything….."

After he listened for a few more minutes and promised to call back with any new developments, he disconnected. Too bad the Jennings sisters would probably never know if John Jennings had been peddling drugs and smuggling people like the truck's original owner. Bo was still trying to figure that out for himself.

He thought about Cassie and her reaction to John's old truck. The Mexican owner had ruined it as a collectible by welding shit on the top of the cab. Bo didn't know many, if any, women who would take it so good naturedly. She was the most positive thinker he had ever met. She was, what had her kids called it? Dope?

With no chairs except the two wooden straight-back chairs at the kitchen table, Cassie and Ronny sat down, side by side on the old lumpy sofa. "*Whew.* What a day," Ronny said. "I'm even more exhausted than yesterday."

"Me, too," Cassie said, "but we made progress."

Ronny chuckled. "Yeah, you got a pair of cowboy boots. Yee-haw."

Cassie held up a foot and inspected the fancy tan boot that struck her mid-calf. It was decorated with colorful tooled flowers. She would have settled for a plainer design, but Ronny had insisted she get the fancy one.

"I've never had a pair of shoes that cost this much money."

"They're fun. You need something fun occasionally."

"We didn't have to spend too much of the cash. And I've still got my pay for January. The next thing we need is to figure out a way to disconnect that music in the pickup so we can get around without causing a spectacle."

"Even if we get the music shut off, I don't see how driving around in a vehicle with a giant taco on top isn't going to cause a spectacle. Do you suppose the old man really made money selling tacos and tamales? Or did he smuggle drugs out of Mexico and sell them here? And advertise himself with that ridiculous pickup?"

"Oh, my gosh, Ronny. I can't stand to think about it. I'm a teacher of young children. For hours a day, I'm their guardian. Parents trust me to guide them in a moral direction as well as teach them the three *R*s.

"I'm not ready to give up yet, but if we found out he was a drug dealer, I would deny the inheritance. I don't want my name associated with a purveyor of illicit drugs that kill people, even in a distant place no one in Tonawilla will ever see. If we find out this is true, I will forfeit my half of the inheritance to you and go back to Tonawilla."

Ronny gasped. "And leave me here all by myself? What makes you think I want it? If you recall, I was skeptical about this trip from the beginning." She heaved a sigh. "There must be someone in this little town who can work the truck over. I wouldn't mind driving it if we got rid of the music and the taco on top. Only a total nut-job would drive around in that monstrosity."

"The will didn't say anything about altering the pickup, did it? Do you suppose that's what our father was? A nut-job?"

"I can't figure it out yet. There are a lot of unanswered questions."

"I know."

Ronny laughed. "Like, how many tacos would you have to sell to make a living? How much does a taco cost? Probably less than a barroom pizza slice."

"I know."

"What do you mean, 'you know'?" You suggested I should learn to make tacos and tamales."

"I was kidding you."

"Think about it," Ronny went on. "We don't even know what our sperm donor who left us in this mess looked like. Too bad we can't ask Mom."

"I still miss her," Cassie replied. "She was so wise."

"My more immediate worry is a washing machine and dryer," Ronny said. "We're going to be running out of clean clothes."

Cassie chuckled. "And that would be a real tragedy for you, Sister."

Ronny sighed again. "We should hit the hay. Tomorrow will be busy, too. You're going to the airport and I'm going to stay here and use our new cleaning supplies to spruce up this place and the two cans of bug spray we bought to exterminate. It should get rid of creepy crawlers."

"I'll make sure we aren't gone all day so I can come back and help you."

"No need to rush back. Take as long as you need to." Ronny got to her feet. "You take the new bed. I've already claimed the old one and it's fine."

The next morning, after scarcely sleeping all night. Cassie dressed with care. She put on the only top she had that hadn't been lying on the asphalt of La Fiesta's parking lot. It was one of her favorites and she felt comfortable wearing it, but it didn't matter because she had to cover it with a sweater. Maybe the temperature would warm up later today. Hadn't she heard someone say once that if you didn't like the weather in Texas, wait ten minutes and it would change?

Bless Ronny for not teasing her about the extra time she had spent on her makeup and clothing.

Besides being good-looking, Bo was the nicest man she had ever met. He appeared to be strong and decisive, yet soft-spoken and gentle. Nothing like Frank who was loud and bossy and always trying to look bigger than he was.

"Stay close to his bumper," Ronny cautioned. "You could get lost in all of this vastness surrounding us." Ronny windmilled her arms.

"The car has GPS. It got us here, didn't it? Besides, Bo will be watching me in his rearview mirror."

"I'm just saying, he might have trouble seeing you. In his rearview mirror, you might look like something his exhaust pipe expelled."

Cassie couldn't keep from chuckling. What would she do without her sister's clever comments?

Bo showed up looking handsome as usual in jeans and a white dress shirt and they set out for the airport in Harlingen.

Ronny stood in the courtyard doorway and watched as Cassie and Bo drove away. The little Smart Car following Bo's enormous pickup looked like a period at the end of a long sentence.

Wrapping her sweater close to her body, she walked back into the house. The cold front was moving out, but the nighttime temperature was still in the fifties.

As it turned out, the water from the well made an excellent cup of coffee. She decided to go for a fourth cup. As she sipped the black brew, her cell phone bleated. Other than Cassie, who in the world could be calling her? She connected. Crackled static came on the line. "This is Ronny. Talk to me."

"Ma'am, this is Tex. Tex Barton."

More static. "Tex Barton! We've been waiting for you to call. Can you hear me?"

"Almost. Are you on top of the barn?"

"What? What are you talking about?"

"You need to find a high place so we can hear each other. The cell tower is between here and Harlingen."

Ronny's mind scrambled. *Top of the barn, top of the house, top of the table under the palm tree in the courtyard.* "Just a minute."

Ronny carried the phone outside and climbed on top of the cast iron patio table. From that vantage point, she could see over the courtyard wall. "Can you hear me now?" she asked Tex.

"That's a little better."

"You're the fixer upper dude Bo told us about, right?"

"Is that what Bo called me? Fixer upper dude?" He chortled. "Maybe I should put that on a business card. That is, if I had a business card." He chortled again.

Ronny took an immediate liking to his easy, laid-back demeanor. "How do people remember you if you don't have a card? I worked at a bar in New York and the walls were papered with business cards."

"And that's pretty much what they're good for. I don't use them because people tend to not forget me."

Uh-oh. Was he full of himself to an obnoxious level? Okay, fine. She had no problem with men like that. In fact, she used them to sharpen her wit and tongue. "You don't say," she said. "You're not one of those misogynistic, egotistic, self-centered, Shut-up-I'm-in-charge kind of assholes, are you?"

He laughed again. "Well, I'm not miso-whatever, egotistic or self-centered, although my ex-wives would probably disagree. Bo said you wanted some remodeling on the old Cervantez place. I suggest you start out with a coat of paint outdoors. An orange house is odd-looking."

At least he hadn't denied being an asshole. Her first

impression was correct. "What color do you suggest?"

"A nice cream color, or latte. Maybe a robin's egg blue."

Ronny's brow creased. She had never lived in an orange house. She was growing fond of orange. "I'll talk to my sister about it. On the work, I don't know if the word remodel is right. Maybe updating is what we're wanting. We don't have a whole lot of money. We want to keep it to the bathroom mostly, maybe the kitchen if there's anything left over, and God knows. the living room could use some help."

"But no remodel. Right. Got it. I'll come out in a day or two and you can show me what you want."

"Do you know how to get here? I can give directions, I think."

"Naw, we're good. I know the place."

"What kind of time frame are we talking about? Do you have other jobs? We're only going to be here a year, so—"

"No problem darlin', I've got seven jobs underway now and about three more in the next month. I can get to you easily."

"Seven jobs?'"

"Sure 'nuff. This is a slow time for me. I'm usually busier than a one-legged cat trying to cover a turd on a hot tin roof." He laughed again.

What the hell had he just said? Speechless, which didn't happen often, Ronny paused.

"Check you later, darlin'," he said and was gone.

Ronny clambered off the patio table, marched back inside, attached the phone to its charger and tasted her coffee. *Damn.* It was cold. She looked around, assessing the chores she needed to finish before

Cassie returned. She gathered the broom, a dustpan she had found in a closet in the kitchen and a can of the aerosol bug spray they had bought yesterday. Armed, she headed for the bathroom.

She hadn't previously seen a yellowed-from-time note taped on a lower corner of the mirror mounted over the vanity. Taking the time to read it, she discovered a list of instructions. She had never needed instructions for showering, but the note was specific: *Don't turn on the shower and any other faucet in the house at the same time. Allow shower to run several minutes before using to allow debris to run out.*

She stopped reading for a few minutes and frowned. *Debris?*

She returned to Item #3: *Wait a good ten minutes after flushing the toilet before you use the shower.*

Number one she could live with, but the second and third wanted to send her screaming and pulling her hair. She and her sister might as well be camped out in a tent outdoors.

Then it dawned on her, this was the perfect time to try the shower. Cassie had managed a shower, but she hadn't. She returned to the living room and dug the new shower curtain rod, rings and shower curtain they had bought yesterday from one of the sacks, she carried all of it to the bathroom to put it together.

Preparing to turn on the water in the shower, she stopped dead in her tracks. A creature, the likes of which she had never seen, occupied the tub. "*Aaiee!* she screamed and jumped back.

Her heart racing, she gathered her courage and took a step forward to see it close. It was black. And gray. And hairy. It had a dozen legs and was the size of the Smart Car Cassie was returning to the airport.

Oh, my God! A tarantula!

She had seen picture of the beast, but she had never seen a real one.

The monster lifted a leg. She screamed again and raced out of the bathroom. Reaching into the plastic shopping bag, she pulled out the two towels they had bought yesterday and stuffed them under the doorway to make sure it didn't escape.

"*Jesus, Joseph and Mary!*" she mumbled her voice wobbly. "What is this, Wild Kingdom?"

So much for a shower. And so much for cleaning the bathroom. She would let King of the Cowboys' deal with the monster when he and Cassie returned. "Texas," she grumbled. "Big deal. Big trucks, big men and big bugs."

This situation didn't need more coffee; after four cups, her caffeine level had soared to the max. What she needed was wine. There was a monster in the tub and the situation called for alcohol.

Just then, she heard the now familiar sound of a large pickup driving up, but it was too soon for Cassie and Bo to be coming back. *Oh, my God!* Mexican bandits. Cartel members coming to chop off her head and take what…the house?

Her heartbeat took off on another wild tangent.

Then, thunderous pounding on the front door. Her adrenaline amped, she jumped and caught her breath.

Gathering her height to its maximum five feet and nine inches, she crept to the door and bellowed. "Who the fuck is it? I've got a gun and my husband has gone to get his, his, uh… crossbow! He's an expert crossbowman!"

The next sound she heard was laughter. *Laughter?* A peep hole to peer through was too much to hope for. A voice she had heard before came through. "Ma'am, this is Tex." More laughter. "We're gonna have to work on your badass delivery while you're here. Crossbow?" Followed by more laughing.

Ronny yanked the door open to a sight she should have been prepared for, but so far, since arriving a little more than forty-eight hours ago, she'd been surprised at every turn.

A massive, muscular man stood before her, dabbing at his eyes with his handkerchief. He had to be at least six-four, maybe five and weighed easily two-ninety. Despite the cooler weather he wore knee-length shorts and a T-shirt that announced to the world, "I'd do me." An orange visor that said "UT" and a mirrored pair of sunglasses perched on his head.

A huge grin tipped up the corners of his mouth. Laughter showed in his eyes. "Hi. I'm Tex Barton."

Miffed at being laughed at, Ronny glared at his hand. "I just got off the phone with you. I didn't expect to see you for days."

"Darlin', the only thing you can expect from me is gratitude, perfection and satisfaction."

"Gee. While we work on my badass delivery, we need to put some time in on your confidence level."

"Hell, darlin', that's a lost cause. I've got four brothers and I'm the timid one. Now, I've got a couple of minutes. Show me what you want done."

Ronny stood back from the door, "You just jump right into it, don't you? Come in."

"Hold on," he said, raising a thick sausage-like finger, "let me get some paper and my pen."

Ronny followed him into the courtyard and watched as he jogged to his pickup, a much larger vehicle than Bo's. The entire body was wrapped in red, white and blue, touting his name and phone number.

"Holy cow. That's quite a paint job. No wonder you don't need business cards."

"It's a vinyl wrap. You should see my boat over at the coast. It's got the same wrap. How cool is that?"

Pulling a receipt from Lotta Liquor out of his pocket, he flipped it over and clicked his pen. "Okay, what are you thinking."

"I'm thinking you don't have enough paper," Ronny said.

"Darlin', I don't have all day. Just tell me what you want."

She started rattling a litany of items, counting off on her fingers: new plumbing in the bathroom, new shower head and faucets, replace toilet and lighting in bathroom, locks for outside doors and check the fireplace to see if it was safe to use. Also, a place for a washing machine and dryer.

She stopped. "You're not writing anything down."

"That's a lot of work, but you said you didn't have a lot of money to spend. Maybe we'd better start with your budget. How much we talkin'?"

Now came the hard part. From being married to lying, cheating Tommy Argyle. Ronny knew what this pitiful place needed would cost way more than the twenty thousand their father had left them. She also knew to start low and inch up but start too high and they would be screwed.

While she pondered, Tex said, "I'll be right up

front." He started counting off on his thick fingers. "That's a no to the new plumbing, shower head, faucets, commode and most everything else you mentioned."

He moved to the next finger. "No to the washing machine and dryer unless you've got a good well and want to spend a boatload of money. When this place was built, they were washing clothes by pounding them on a wet rock in the river. The place ain't wired for a dryer either. In other words, there are a lot of people in Cameron County who think this place oughtta be tore down."

Inside, Ronny winced. She suspected as much. "I'm not pounding my clothes on a wet rock. Where are we supposed to do our laundry?"

"I thought you just got here. You got dirty clothes already?"

"Our clothes got spread all over the parking lot at La Fiesta drive-up place in Harlingen."

He gave her a flat look, his big grin gone. "I'm not even gonna ask what that was about. Look, the grocery store in town's got a coin-operated washing machine and a dryer in the back room. Be sure to take a bag full of quarters with you."

Okay, moving on, Ronny thought. Embarrassed to reveal their paltry funds to this affable stranger, she spoke up with bravado. "Back to the work on the place, what can we get for two hundred?"

Tex tilted his head back and cackled. "For two hundred you can probably get a really nice shower curtain and some matching towels with maybe a throw rug if it's all on sale."

Ronny loved entertaining and making people

laugh; she wasn't so good at being mocked herself. "We've already got that. I'm not accustomed to being told no so many times by a man. Surely we can compromise on some of it."

"Oh, no, you don't," Tex said, waving his thick forefinger like a pendulum. "Don't you flirt with me and break my heart. I've been married three times and—"

"Hah. Me, too."

"That so? Well, lemme tell you, I know a little something about getting married and unmarried. The next woman in my life, I'm gonna cut out all the bullshit and just give her half my money and my house and go on to the next one. And there's always a next one, darlin'."

Ronny stood dumbfounded and confused. She was never at a loss for words. She wasn't sure if she should laugh, recount some of her own horror stories with marriage and divorce or simply tell him to leave.

Before she could say more, he walked over to the bathroom, bent down and dragged the towels away from the bathroom door. "Whatcha got trapped in here, a mouse?"

"A very large spider. Not your run of the mill spider at all. I'd appreciate it if you'd kill it."

"Kill it?" His chin ducked and he gave her a frown. "Oh, my. That's awful violent, darlin' Has it hurt anybody?"

"Not yet, but it looks like it could."

He walked into the bathroom and peered into the tub. He bent down and allowed the tarantula to walk up onto his palm, then up his arm.

Ronny scurried out and to the other side of the

kitchen as Tex headed to the front door. "What are you going to do with it?"

"I'm gonna turn it loose." He walked on out to the courtyard, put his hand down and allowed the spider to walk onto the ground.

He straightened. "I'll get back to you in a day or two on the stuff you wanted. I'm a little bit short-handed. I won't be able to do it all, but I promise you'll get—"

"I know. Gratitude, perfection and satisfaction. I have another question. On the remodeling, what if I helped you? And you could give us credit for the work I do."

He lifted off his cap and scratched his bald head. "I don't know about that, darlin'. Do you know a hammer from a nail?"

"Of course I do. Didn't I say I was married to a builder? I used to help him. I'm hell-for-stout at installing tile. And painting? I can cut in a line as thin as a razor blade."

His squinted eyes settled on hers. "I always need a little help. Let me think about it."

CHAPTER 9

AFTER TEX HAD gotten rid of the spider and left for one of his jobs, Ronny set about cleaning with a fevered diligence. As she wiped the kitchen counters with Clorox, she thought about job prospects, which seemed to amount to zilch. That is, unless Tex would hire her. She had liked helping her ex-husband, the builder. She hadn't like him so much, but she liked the work.

As soon as she had made the place as sparkling as possible, she gathered their new bottle of laundry detergent, the clothing she and Cassie had picked up off the asphalt at La Fiesta, stuffed it all into a pillowcase and set out for Lost Tropicos.

Remembering the lawyer's advice, outside she searched for a suitable stick she could use to scare off a snake. She found a broken branch waist high and two inches thick. On the way to the barn, she beat and swept at the grass.

Getting the taco truck out of the barn proved to be no easy task. Struggling with the four-in-the floor transmission, she would have crashed through the back of the barn if bales of hay hadn't stopped her.

With a growl of gears, she found reverse and leapt backward out of the barn. After numerous stops and starts and screeks, she got the truck going forward. The lack of power steering didn't help matters much. Now she understood why a knob that looked like a doorknob was attached the steering wheel.

Finally, she headed for *Lost* Tropicos with loud trumpets and guitars and a song in Spanish blaring for miles around. *Ay-ay-ay*..... She willed herself not to hear it.

At the grocery store, a man at the only check-out counter said matter-of-factly, "You're driving John Jennings' old truck. I heard you coming. For a minute there, I thought John had made a reappearance." He raised his hands and squiggled his fingers.

Dummy, she thought.

"So who are you?" he asked.

Anxiety passed through Ronny as she spotted a pistol on the man's belt. *Does everyone in Texas wear a gun?* she wanted to ask, but she said nervously, "Ronny Jennings. I'm John Jennings' daughter. Or one of them, that is. My sister and I inherited his stuff. We came down here to check it out. We live in New York."

"New York City?"

"Upstate. A small town. Tonawilla."

"I never knew John had any kids." The man put out his right hand. "Clay Thompson."

Ronny shook hands.

"I own this fine establishment." Thompson gestured in a circle with his hand. "It's kind of the center of town. Sooner or later, everybody who lives in Los Tropicos comes in here, either to pick up a few groceries or eat in the café or mail a package. We've got the best Tex-Mex food for miles. Also a little post office and we're a pickup for UPS.

"Got a nice little RV park, too. It's got a comfortable shower and bathroom facility. It's handy for the snowbirds who winter down here in their RVs."

"I heard about the snowbirds."

"Town meetings and elections take place here, too. And anything else that calls for people to get together."

"Can other people besides the ones in RVs use that shower."

"We don't encourage public use. Why do you ask?"

"The bathroom in our house isn't great. The shower's corroded and I don't know when we'll be able to get it fixed. If I could use your shower to wash my hair, I'd be grateful."

"Guess we could make an exception for a neighbor. I'll get you the key."

"I heard you had some washing machines and dryers."

"We do. That what you're looking for? Follow me." He started toward the back of the store. "You and your sister gonna be living here now?"

Revealing too many details of her dad's will to this Clay Thompson didn't seem like a good idea. He had an "information central" air about him.

"Uh, we don't know yet," Ronny answered, lugging the pillowcase stuffed with her and Cassie's clothes. "You were friends with our dad?"

"I knew him is all. Sometimes I bought tamales from him to re-sell here in the store. People love homemade tamales, you know."

"No, I don't know. I never ate one." She set her pillowcase on the floor in front of one of a washing machine. "I need some quarters." She dug in her satchel and came up with a twenty.

Thompson took the bill. "Be right back." He hurried away.

While she waited for quarters, Ronny stuffed their laundry into the washing machine. Thompson soon returned with two rolls of quarters and a key to the bathroom facility.

"Our dad really did that, huh?" she asked. "Made tacos and tamales? He made a living doing that?"

Thompson braced his back against the door jamb, his arms crossed over a barrel chest. "I used to wonder about that myself. Don't know if he made 'em himself. A Mexican woman lived with him for a while. I always suspected she was the one who made the tamales.

"Not just anybody can make good tamales and the ones he sold were good. Saved my wife some work. Now, the guy who owned that truck before John was a Mexican from Mexico. He made tacos and tamales alright, but he passed on."

This conversation was growing more interesting. "How did my dad end up with his truck?"

"That's a good question. I don't know anybody around here who knows the answer to that. I just know John had a lot of contacts in Mexico."

Ronny made a mental note. A question for Bo when he and Cassie returned.

"You wouldn't know anyone who could take that sign off the top of the truck and get rid of the music, would you?"

"You'd have to find somebody in Harlingen to do that. You staying in the house?"

Ronny chose her answer carefully. "While we're here."

A chime sounded from the front of the store. Thompson pushed away from the jamb and scanned the store, then returned his attention to Ronny. "Newspaper delivery from Harlingen. Comes in daily. You interested in the newspaper?"

Why would I be interested in a Harlingen newspaper? "Uh, no."

"So, uh, is that fireplace in John's house talking to you yet?" He followed the question with a heh-heh-heh.

A visual of the oversize fireplace crudely constructed of bricks and plaster came into Ronny's mind. "What do you mean?"

"I never was in John's house, so I've never seen that fireplace. But some folks around here think it's haunted. A couple of people I'm acquainted with have heard voices and other noises coming from inside it."

The hair raised on Ronny's arms. She didn't believe in ghosts, but still...

"The sheriff over in Harlingen told me the DPS thinks it's a route for smuggling illegals and drugs," Thompson continued. "Like I said, I've never been in the place myself, so I really don't know."

Ronny's stomach began to tremble. *Shit.* What had she and Cassie gotten into? "What kind of drugs? And what is DPS?"

"The bad kind. 'Course it's all bad. Cocaine and Fentanyl, I heard. That's why you see guys from DPS hanging around here. They eat in the café from time to time. DPS stands for Department of Public Safety. State cops. That Fentanyl is poison and it's killing people."

Ronny's need to talk to her sister became all-consuming. "Look, I need to finish up here. If we find any ghosts living in the fireplace, I'll let you know."

"Right," Thompson said. Taking the hint, he strolled back into the grocery store.

Ronny found a chair and sat, waiting for the washing machine to finish. Anxiety had her knee jumping up and down and her heel drumming the floor.

Remembering what her sister had said last night, they might be on their way back to Tonawilla way sooner than a year from now. That was okay. This place was like a bad western movie. Mike Duffy was still holding a bartending job for her in Duffy's Tavern in Tonawilla and Cassie still had her teaching job at Blueberry Elementary. They might forfeit the house and land but they still had more than half of twenty-thousand dollars to take back with them.

Ronny transferred the clothing from the washing machine to the dryer and shoved in six quarters. Then she bought a couple of small bottles of shampoo and conditioner from the store and headed for a shower in the RV bathroom facility.

When she returned, the grocery store owner met her with a Walmart sack in his hand. "I kept an eye on your clothes. They're finished drying."

"Thanks." She handed the bathroom facility key back to him. "And thanks for letting me use that shower. It was a lifesaver."

"I told my wife we had new folks in town. She wanted to come over and meet you, but you were outside." He extended his arm with the Walmart sack. "She made you some brisket tacos. I told her you've never eaten a tamale, so she threw a couple of those in, too"

"Brisket. We had that yesterday. Is that what everybody here eats?"

"If they can. She made some guacamole and some tortillas, too. She's the best cook around. She runs the café."

"Thanks again," Ronny said and took the sack. "Tell her how much we appreciate it."

"It's her way of thanking you for what John did for so many."

Now Ronny was confused by the mixed signals surrounding their father. "Oh, yeah? He was a good guy?"

Thompson made a rocking motion with his hand. "Depends on who you ask."

Before he could say more, Ronny's phone bleated. "Hey, Cass. What's up?"

"We're almost home."

It wasn't lost on Ronny that Cassie said the word "home." Ronny had a long way to go before she would call an orange stucco house in the Texas outback "home."

"Bo wants to show us around the land," Cassie went on. "He says that if we've never seen a longhorn cow, it's time we did. Do you want to go with us?"

"I'll leave the exploring to you and Cowboy Casanova. I'm still in town finishing up the laundry, then I'm headed back to the house. There's a shower here we can use in the RV park. Oh, and the guy that owns the store brought us a sack of tacos and tamales. Apparently, that's the local menu. He said it was his wife's way of thanking us for what our dad has done. What do you think that means?"

"I have no idea. Maybe he did something nice for her one time. Bo and I will be at the house pretty soon."

Ronny folded the dried laundry and stacked it neatly in the pillowcase, eager to get on the road. It would be dark soon and she wouldn't be able to see where she was going. *Lost* Tropicos' one streetlight was strategically placed in front of the grocery store/café/service station. No lights existed anywhere else and none on the road back to the house. Ronny was comfortable with turn-by-turn directions, but she feared getting lost in the dark.

As she drove, she noticed the sunset. Back home in New York, the setting sun gradually sank behind the mountains, leaving layers of color and light in its wake. Here, the big golden ball behaved as if it had been pricked with a pin. It was there in all of its splendor in one minute, then, pop. It was gone.

She drove like the Hounds of Hell were chasing her so she could get to get to the house before she was left in total darkness. The faster she drove, the faster and louder the damn music played. When she crossed the cattleguard, she breathed a sigh of relief. She was only a few miles from the house.

Once there, she rejected parking the taco truck in the barn. She didn't relish wading through the tall grass at twilight to get to the house's back door. Texas had varmints she had never even considered.

She parked in front of the doorway leading into the courtyard. On the ground beside the doorway, she saw a couple of cans of paint and some sacks from Home Depot. So Tex had been here.

She unlocked the door, wishing she had left a light on. She picked up the sacks Tex had left and crossed the courtyard to the house's front door. With her hands full, she reached inside, fumbling for the light switch.

The light came on, she stepped inside and set the pillowcase and Home Depot sacks on the beat-up kitchen table. As she turned to go back to the courtyard for the cans of paint, her gaze landed on the old sofa. Two young girls huddled together, staring at her.

She yelped and jumped back. They screamed; one cried.

She bolted outside, all the way across the courtyard to the taco truck. Her heart pounding, she dug in her satchel for her phone. She could think of only one person to call.

Tex Barton's booming voice came on the line. "What's up, darlin'?"

"Help! How close are you? I need help."

A deep throated chuckled crossed the line. "You got another monster to deal with? A bug in the tub?"

"How about a gal and her pal? I just came home from town and two women, well, more like young girls, are in the house."

"What do you mean 'in the house'? Even the courtyard door was locked when I came by earlier with a few supplies."

"I locked both doors before I went to town."

"What were they doing?"

"Nothing. They're just parked on the couch like they're waiting for a bus. Just sitting there staring at me. They've got a backpack."

"Where are they now? Did you scare 'em off?"

"They're still in the house. Please come help me. I don't know if they speak English. I don't know if they're armed. I don't know anything except I'm not getting out of this truck."

"The taco truck? Why're you in the taco truck?"

Ronny was about to lose her mind. "It doesn't matter why I'm in the friggin' truck," she yelled. "Can you please just come and help me? Or should I call nine-one-one?"

"Nine-one-one calls go to the sheriff's office in Harlingen. No need to get those limp dicks involved. It'll take 'em an hour to get here and they turn everything into an international crisis. It'll be on the news next thing you know. I'm not ten minutes from you. See you in a few." He disconnected.

"Don't hang up!" Ronny yelled into emptiness.

She struck the steering wheel with the wheel of her hand. Dammit, she wished he had stayed on the line. Now she would have to hold her breath for ten minutes until he got here.

In what seemed like mere minutes, she heard the deafening—but comforting—roar of his monster pickup. From out of the darkness, a shadowy image of the vehicle emerged. A bar of lights customized to fit the top lit the whole area around them as bright as daylight.

He came to an abrupt stop behind the taco truck, spewing dirt in a halo around the pickup. Ronny fought the instinct to rush to him and throw her arms around his neck. She had to remind herself that she wasn't a girly-girl from the city. She could handle this.

Now that he was here.

He stepped down from the pickup, hiking up his jeans. "They still inside?"

"Yes," she answered shakily. "I haven't taken my eyes off this door."

"Well, darlin', I don't know what you're accomplishing watching this door. It's just a door to the courtyard. What about the front door to the house? What about the back door?"

The back door. *Shit!* She hadn't even thought about the back door. "Are—are you going inside?"

"Would you rather I stand out here and yell for them to come out? You said they were young. Kids, probably. If you're scared, imagine how *they* feel."

"I don't care how they feel. You don't expect to come home and find strangers in your house." Ronny lifted her nose in defiance. "I'm not scared. I was just startled."

"Well, darlin', they're sure to be *startled,* too. So lets go inside quietly and see what this is all about."

"Do you have a gun? Don't all Texans have guns?"

"I do. And a lot of others do, too."

"Are you going to carry it with you?"

He gave her a patient look. "I'm not. You comin'?"

He opened the door and cautiously entered the courtyard. Ronny fell in step behind him, his big body blocking her view. "Hello, inside the house," he called out. "We want to help you. Come out, wherever you are." He followed that with what she assumed was the same speech in Spanish.

No response. Tex warily opened the front door exposing the living room. Ronny followed him into both bedrooms and the bathroom. He pushed back the shower curtain. Then, they walked back to the kitchen. He opened the backdoor and looked outside. They found nothing or nobody.

"Darlin', are you sure—"

"Of course, I'm sure. Positive." She pointed to the sofa. "They were sitting right there on this sofa."

He planted his hands on his hips. "Well, I'm thinking that when you left, they did, too. Must've gone out the back door."

"Oh, God. You mean they're out there? In this dark cave? We have to find them."

"I'll drive around a little bit. See if I can spot 'em. You wanna ride? Two sets of eyes are better than one."

With terror filling her heart, no way did she want to stay alone in this house in the middle of nowhere. "Yes!"

"Could you tell if they were Mexicans?" he asked as they walked back to his pickup. He opened the passenger side door.

All at once, Ronny was as puzzled as she was afraid. "Oh, my God. They weren't Mexicans. They were white. What does that mean?"

"Are you sure?"

"I'm sure."

"Hm. Caucasian girls. That is interesting….Well, get in. Let's go."

Ronny climbed onto the passenger seat. Tex rounded the frontend and climbed behind the wheel.

"If the doors were locked, how did they get in?" Ronny asked, still nervous.

"Don't know. If they're on foot, hope they've got water and food."

A light blinked in Ronny's brain. The sack of food Clay Thompson had given her was gone. "I don't know about water, but they've got food. Mr. Thompson sent a sack of tacos and tamales his wife made home with me. I put it on the table. When you and I went through the house? It wasn't there."

"Are you saying they stole Elena Thompson's tacos and tamales? That does it. Now, we're calling the law. Elena makes the best Mexican food in Cameron County. People drive down here from Harlingen to eat. If Clay lost her, that café would be out of business."

CHAPTER 10

B Y THE TIME Ronny and Tex returned to the house, Cassie and Bo were there. Adrenaline running high, Ronny quickly told them all that had happened. She concluded by saying, "And we don't know how they got in."

Through it all, Tex said little and Bo said nothing.

Ronny gave her sister a direct look, eye-to-eye. "I'm holding you to what you said yesterday."

Cassie didn't often show a stubborn streak, but her jaw clenched. "This doesn't make me ready to just give up."

Before Ronny could say more, Tex put in, "I've run out of ideas on this, but I don't think it's a ghost." He looked at Bo. "You're a neighbor. You got any thoughts?"

"Uh, well….Uh, no….But I don't think we should jump to conclusions. In this part of Texas, this close to the border, it's not uncommon for illegals to show up in homes."

Ronny shot him a bug-eyed glare. "What the hell is that supposed to mean? That we should just expect

people to break into our house at any time? And
that's okay?"

Bo met her steely gaze with one of his own. "Surely
you have break-ins or home invasions in New York.
This is no different."

"There's a big difference. Back home, thieves are
usually from this country and speak English. And
we'd know how they got in. Here, they just appear
like dust on the furniture and are gone like that." She
snapped her fingers.

Tex spoke up again. "Look, darlin', we've done all
we can do with it being nighttime and all. I need to
get going. I've got an early day tomorrow on a job
site."

He reset his gimme cap. "But you know? How
those girls got in here is bugging me. I'll be over here
tomorrow afternoon to let you girls know what I
think you oughtta do to this place to make it a little
more livable and we'll go over everything with a fine-
toothed comb. See if we can figure it out. Everything
looks different in the daylight."

He started for the door. "You girls try to get a good
night's sleep. Be sure you lock your doors."

With that, he was gone.

Bo, too, stammered that he needed to get home.
"But I'm not comfortable leaving y'all here alone,"
he added at the last minute. "If y'all don't mind, I'll
just stay here tonight. I'll, uh, sleep on the couch.
That way, if anybody comes in, I'll see them."

Ronny and Cassie stared at each other, silently
asking, *Is that okay?*

When they didn't object, he said, "I'm just gonna

go outside and get my sleeping bag and lock up my truck."

He left through the front door, slamming the door behind himself.

"That was weird," Ronny said, "him stuttering around like that. Did you think that was weird?"

Cassie dropped to a seat at the rustic kitchen table, an expression of bewilderment on her face. "Thank goodness he's staying. If we were here alone, I don't think I could sleep a wink."

"Bo knows something he's not telling," Ronny said. "If he didn't, why would he volunteer to spend the night here?"

Ronny took the seat opposite Cassie at the rustic kitchen table. "Cassie, listen to me. There's some kind of crazy shit going on here and it has nothing to do with us. It could even be dangerous. We need to get the hell out of here. Let's get our stuff repacked and use that return trip ticket. We could be gone in a flash."

"There must be someone who can figure it out."

"Cassie, I don't want someone to figure it out. You don't know how it felt when I walked in here and saw those two strange girls. I want to go home."

"This *is* home, Ronny. Even with all the obstacles we're facing, I still feel better here than I did in Tonawilla. I feel like we own something. The land looks nice. There's so much of it. And it's all covered with grass. Think about it, Ronny. Eighty acres. I never dreamed that someday we would own a city lot, let alone eighty acres."

"BFD," Ronny barked. "What good is eighty acres in the middle of nowhere? What do we own, really?

A hundred-year-old concrete shack that needs a ton of work and barely has running water?"

"We have the cows."

"And they're probably old and crippled."

"They don't look old and crippled. Have you ever seen a longhorn cow?"

Ronny lifted her nose defiantly. "Of course I have. One of those guys who comes into Duffy's at home had a picture in his wallet."

"That's not the same as seeing one for real. They're magnificent, Ronny. Their horns are so wide I don't think they'd fit in this room."

"And that's a reason to stay here?"

Cassie's eyes glistened with tears. "We've only been here three days. We haven't given it a fair chance. I'm not ready to go back to Tonawilla."

Ronny couldn't stand to see her little sister cry. She heaved a great sigh, willing to give up the fight for the time being. "Okay, okay, I get it. I don't like it, but I get it."

Just then, Bo returned, carrying a sleeping bag and halting their conversation.

The next morning Cassie was the last to awaken. She was still catching up on sleep after having little for three days and nights. She entered the kitchen and found Ronny and Bo talking and laughing over coffee. A pang of emotion she couldn't identify shot through her.

Their conversation immediately stopped when she

walked into the room. Headed for the coffee pot, she gave them both a stern look. "Were you two talking about me? Don't forget I'm teacher of young children. Conversation gone to silence is practically taught when we're in college."

She carried her mug of coffee to the table. Bo rose quickly and pulled out a chair for her. He was beautiful, even needing a shave and his wavy hair sticking out every which way. "Thank you."

He sat back down.

"Speaking of teaching," Ronny said, "Bo was just educating me about the cattle business."

"Wish I had been awake," Cassie replied. "I suppose we need to know about that now that we've got the cows."

"We'll have to discuss that," Ronny said.

Bo rose, picked up his hat and the satchel he had brought in last night. "I need to get home. It's rare for me to spend the night away. I've got a couple of horses and dog to feed and some cattle of my own." He started for the door.

Cassie quickly got to her feet. "I'll walk with you."

She went with him outside, without a sweater or jacket. The cold front had passed through. The sun was shining and the temperature was in the seventies. "I love the sunshine," she told him. "When we left home, the temperature was minus two."

"Can't beat wintertime here," Bo said. "Makes living here worthwhile."

"It's nice out here," Cassie said, running her fingers over the rusted wrought-iron table.

"Yes, ma'am. A good place for morning coffee."

"I know. I want to take the rust off this table and chairs and paint it."

Bo nodded and continued to the courtyard exit. Before he opened the door, he looked down at her. "Cassie, I don't want you to worry. We'll get to the bottom of this."

She tilted her face up, seeing sincerity in his eyes. "I know you will."

"I'll be back this afternoon to see what Tex has to say."

She closed her eyes, feeling that a good-bye kiss was inevitable only to open them again when she heard the door open.

"I'll, see you later," he said, and he was gone. Cassie wanted to break down and cry.

Ronny appeared at her side. "That man is totally taken with you."

"Hah. He doesn't even want to kiss me." Cassie pushed her sister out of the way. "I was just left with my eyes closed and my lips pursed like a fish on the end of a line and you say he's taken with me? And he rarely spends the night away from his home, I wonder what other rare occasions he has and with whom."

"God," Ronny said, smiling, "you two are just too damn cute. I've seen the looks between you. Time to fire up the old Bunsen burner."

Cassie's cheeks flushed. "Don't say those things. They aren't true. And I do have someone back in Tonawilla."

"Frank? Is that a joke? You're planning on staying here. Are you going to move him down here, too?"

"I don't know. I haven't thought about it yet."

"All I can say is Bo Buckaroo or Bugaboo or

Buckalew, or whatever his name is, scrapes crap off his boots that's better than Frank Kowalski. Have you even talked to that drip since we got here?"

"We've been so busy. He called, but I wasn't where I could take the call. Bo and I—"

"Ah. You already had a choice and you made it. I'm telling you, Sister, you should be all over Bo, like shit on a diaper."

Cassie closed her eyes and shook her head. "That is not a pretty picture. You kill me."

"Don't tempt me."

"Let's go back inside and get some lunch. I've got an idea I want to tell you about."

"*Oh, hell.* One of your ideas is how we got into this mess in the first place."

"It isn't a mess, Ronny. We just have a few problems to solve."

Leaving the Jennings sisters, Bo pressed a stored number on his phone and put it on speaker as he drove. An answer came after the first burr.

"Hey, Pete. We've had an incident in the Jennings house."

"Tell me about it."

"Two young women appeared while the sisters were away from the house, then disappeared as if by magic."

"Were they Mexicans?"

"I didn't see them, but Ronny Jennings says they were white."

"ICE picked up two young women just out of

Harlingen. They were white. Russian citizens. It's probably them. So far, all we know is they were in Mexico and a man took them there."

"Where are they now?"

"Catholic church in San Antone. They were kidnapped in Massachusetts over a year ago. They've been abused. Both raped. Sold a couple of times. People just don't realize how much at-risk girls and young women are. You say they broke into the Jennings house?"

"I don't know if you can label it a break-in. I suspect they came in somehow through that fireplace, but I don't know how. But the fact that they ended up in the Jennings house means someone directed them to it."

"We still haven't figured out who that person is."

"Somehow, I've got to prowl around inside that fireplace."

"Can't you just tell them what you need to do and do it?"

"Not without blowing my cover. I'm convinced these two sisters don't know anything about what their old man was doing. Remember the carpenter I told you about a couple of days ago? He's coming over this afternoon to discuss work that needs to be done on the house. Maybe between him and me, we can find how people are getting in. He might be persuaded to recommend that they tear down the fireplace. You think the State of Texas would pay him to do that?"

"Sure. Just let me know how much so I can request the funds."

"Good. I'll have to ask the sisters for permission. I

don't think that'll be a problem. The old thing is a fire hazard anyway."

"Keep me posted. We want to capture those kidnappers. One of those girls is in real bad shape."

CHAPTER 11

IN THE KITCHEN, Ronny slathered two tortillas with mayonnaise and slapped them onto two paper plates. "Okay. Hit me with it, Einstein. What's your idea?"

Cassie ignored her sister's sarcasm. "What are you making?"

"I'm calling this ham burrito sandwiches."

"We have groceries now. Why aren't we cooking something?"

Ronny added slices of lunchmeat to each tortilla and rolled them into two neat tubes. "The answer to that question, Sister, is dishpan hands. We may have groceries and even a few pots and pans, but what we do not have is a dishwasher."

Cassie related. She, too, disliked washing pots and pans.

Ronny carried the paper plates and two sheets of paper towel to the table and plopped onto a chair. "Sit down and tell me your idea. I'm all ears."

Cassie took an adjacent chair. "We could start a cow herd. I was thinking we should let our cows have babies. Then we'd have eight."

Picking up her sandwich, Ronny gave her sister the squint-eye. "Are you kidding me? I'm willing to let you be queen of the rodeo, but if you think you're going to build a herd with those four cows, you'd better think again." Ronny bit down on her sandwich. "Those cows are steers," she mumbled around a mouthful of food.

Cassie, too, picked up her sandwich. "So?"

Ronny wiped her mouth with her paper towel. "They're boys, Sister. Not only are they boys, they're *castrated* boys."

Stunned, Cassie felt her eyes bug. "Well—well," she sputtered. "I don't know what to say. Does that mean what I think it does?"

"Yep. They cut off their balls."

"Why would they be castrated?"

"It's what ranchers do to boy calves they're going to sell for meat. Apparently, after they get clipped, the meat is better. Don't ask me why or how. They neuter them when they're little and sell them when they're a year or so old. Don't you remember Mr. Atwater saying our dad had saved them from slaughter?"

"Who told you they were castrated?"

"Bo. This morning when we were drinking coffee. We were talking about what we're ever going to do with them since we can't sell them. I can't believe he didn't tell you when you were out with him yesterday."

Cassie's shoulders lifted in a great sigh. "I think he did. But I thought he meant a type of cow, like Holsteins or Jerseys and so forth. If they can't have babies, what good are they?"

"They're pets, like a dog or cat. Of course, a dog

or cat doesn't need a whole big field for a home and costs a lot less to feed. And you sure can't cuddle something with horns four feet long."

"But—but…"

All at once, a frown grew between Cassie's brows. She laid her head on the table and sobbed.

Ronny petted her hair. "Don't cry, Cassie. Please…. It's okay….Come on. Don't cry. You're my little sister. You know I can't stand to see you cry."

Cassie's disappointment was boundless, but she raised her head, her cheeks and eyes wet. She picked up a sheet of paper towel and blew her nose. "Can't anything ever go right?" she blubbered. "Everything we do is wrong."

"Well—well, look at it this way. At least we won't starve. The old man's will might say we can't sell those animals, but it doesn't say we can't eat them."

Cassie wailed into the paper towel. "I don't want to eat them. I couldn't."

"Look, let's change the subject. Let's fire up that taco truck and go to town. While we're there, we can take a shower and wash our hair in the little RV park's bathroom and talk to that Clay Thompson about Wi-Fi. One of us has to have an income. We need to get you where you can teach and I don't think you want to do it from the barn roof."

"That's silly," Cassie said, wiping her eyes and blowing her nose again. "Why would I even try that?"

Ronny closed her eyes and shook her head. "Never mind."

Cassie wiped her eyes and nose again. "If we go to town, we need to get back here soon. Bo and Tex are coming over. Bo wants to show you the cows."

"Did I say I wanted to see them?"

"Ronny, please be nice. He wants to show them to you and I want you to see them."

"Fine. But right now, what I'd rather see is a sim card and three bars on my phone."

Cassie frowned at her. "I don't know what you just said, but okay. Let's go to town."

She got to her feet and gathered body wash, shampoo and towels. Driving twelve miles to take a bath was ridiculous. They needed their own bathroom shower working.

"You've driven the truck, so you drive," she told Ronny. "And we want to be sure all doors are locked."

"Right," Ronny agreed.

They exited the back door. Ronny grabbed the broom and beat and swept a pathway to the barn. Finally, they mounted the taco truck. Ronny fired the engine, followed by a loud *screeek* as she searched for first gear.

"You said you knew how to drive a *stick*."

"What I said was trying to *learn* how to drive a stick had a lot to do with my third divorce."

"I thought you got a divorce because Tommy Argyle cheated."

"That, too."

A few of Ronny's favorite cusswords, a few jolting halts and starts and a few leaps later, they headed for Los Tropicos, the trumpets and guitars of "*El Rancho Grande*" splintering the air.

"One thing I noticed," Ronny yelled above the noise, "the faster we go, the louder the music gets."

"Then slow down. This is ridiculous," Cassie yelled back. "Tell me again why we're going all the way into town to talk to Mr. Thompson about Wi-fi. Can't we just call him or ask Bo or Tex?"

"You haven't made a single call since we got here, have you?"

A twinge of guilt pinched Cassie because she hadn't called Frank since arriving. She hadn't even returned the calls he had made to her. "No, I haven't."

"You have to be standing on top of something to get a signal," Ronny said. "I stood on top of that table in the courtyard when I talked to Tex. He's the one who suggested the top of the barn."

Cassie crossed her arms over her breasts. "Humph. We don't even have a ladder."

Ronny rolled her eyes. "Mr. Thompson seems like he's pretty sharp. He has his finger in every business in town and just maybe his wife has left some more food around. I've been thinking about those tacos and tamales those girls stole and I'm starving. I've never had a tamale. I had my mouth set on trying it."

In town, they saw a man sweeping the sidewalk in front of the store/cafe. "That's him," Ronny said.

Instantly, Cassie spotted a pistol strapped to his belt. "Oh, my gosh. He's wearing a gun."

"I guess it's not a big deal. People do that down here."

With both hands, the knob on the steering wheel and great effort, she herded the taco truck the curb, standing on both the clutch and the brake to come to a stop. "We made it." She broke into a laugh. "This damn thing doesn't have power steering, you know. Or power brakes. Or air conditioning either."

Mr. Thompson stopped his sweeping and came over to the truck. Ronny cranked down the window.

"Ladies," he said.

"Hi, Clay. Hey, we need Wi-Fi."

"Wi-Fi, huh? Lemme see. Is that what they call it when you connect to the Internet? My youngest son told me he wasn't coming home again until I got that. I told him to do whatever he needed to do to fix it. He made a dozen phone calls and now I get that and we've got lots more TV channels. And my sweetie keeps the Amazon truck busy delivering."

"The Amazon truck comes here?"

"Sure does. Every day, just about."

"Is Internet expensive?"

"I don't have a clue. My bookkeeper pays the bills. All I know is it's worked for us for a long time now."

"I don't suppose your wife made any more tacos or tamales?"

Mr. Thompson chuckled. "You New York girls. Have you eaten all I gave you already?"

Ronny told him the story of finding the two young girls in the living room and how no one seemed to know how they got there. Also, they had stolen the food before she and Cassie even got a tase of it.

Mr. Thompson's smile quickly faded. His brow furrowed and he looked around before leaning closer and speaking in a low voice. "Do not repeat that story to anyone, you understand? There are things that go on around here that young ladies such as yourselves don't need to get involved with."

"It's no secret. Bo and Tex were there and—"

"That's good. You keep them there whenever you can and don't answer the door for anybody. You never know who you're talking to in this part of Texas. Best to keep things to yourself. Hear me?"

His ominous tone raised the hairs on the back of Cassie's neck.

"We promise," Ronny said.

"Do you girls have a gun?"

"Uh, no. We don't know how to shoot."

"I suggest you arm yourselves. Get a gun and learn how to use it. There's no cops around here except when the DPS guys come in to eat and a sheriff's deputy only shows up in an emergency. There's a sporting goods store in Harlingen where—"

"Clay, you're scaring us," Ronny said. "We can't see ourselves in a shoot-out with someone."

He straightened and adjusted his glasses. "Oh. Sorry."

"So, uh, would you mind if we come in the laundromat and use your Wi-Fi? Apparently, I need to call a service and get it hooked up for us."

"Not at all," Mr. Thompson said, the stern demeanor now gone. "Pull in over there and come on in."

Ronnie started the taco truck again and herded it into a parking lot beside the building. "*Shit.* Why do I feel like a teenager that just got caught and I'm grounded?"

"That was cryptic," Cassie said. "What was he talking about? Do we need a gun?"

"I don't know about that, but there are two good things that have already come out of this trip to town. We know there is access to the Internet even at the end of the world and Amazon delivery knows where we are, too."

Two hours and half-a-dozen phone calls later, Cassie and Ronny were back in the taco truck and headed home.

"I cannot believe we can't get connected, Ronny railed, hitting the steering wheel with the heel of her hand. "This is the United States of America, forgodsake. Everyone is supposed to have access to the Internet."

"But it'll work out, Ronny. Have faith." Cassie almost believed her own words.

The orange adobe house came into view.

"That house against this landscape looks like a mistake some artist made painting a picture," Ronny said.

The monster trucks belonging to Bo and Tex were parked in front of the house, sending a wave of warmth all over Cassie. She felt that with one or both of these men anything was possible.

As Ronny brought the taco truck to a stop next to the pickups, Cassie checked her reflection in the mirror, pushed a curl into place and grabbed her purse. Ronny had already left the pickup and was striding into the courtyard. Bo and Tex were sitting at the rusted patio table under one of the palm trees.

"Guess who the world wide web never heard of," Ronny exclaimed. "Cassie and me. I called them all"—she checked off a list on her fingers—"AT&T, Verizon, T-Mobile, Cricket and Virgin. They all but laughed at me. We're not even on the map."

"You called phone companies," Bo said with a soft chuckle. "That was your first mistake."

"In this area, darlin', you're gonna have to use satellite," Tex said.

"Ha-ha," Ronny quipped. "And how are we going to get a satellite? Isn't that what the phone companies use?"

"Yes and no. They use satellite for their signals but for phone and Internet, this far out, you'll have to have a thirty-foot pole with a dish."

"A dish of what," Cassie asked and immediately wished she hadn't. She couldn't seem to stop saying stupid things in Bo's presence. "Oh wait, a dish. Got it."

"I would've had it done before you got here if I'd known you were going to stay," Bo said.

"With a little help from Bo, I can set you a pole," Tex said. "It'll be a couple of weeks before I get to it. Meanwhile, y'all call Rural Satellite Link tomorrow and make an appointment for a dish."

"But I have to start teaching classes a week from today," Cassie said.

"You can come over to my place and do your classes there," Bo put in. "It's just a short drive."

"Thank you so much, but I couldn't impose on you like that. It would be every day. My classes start at eight o'clock in New York. That would be seven o'clock here. It would be a huge inconvenience for you."

"I don't mind," he said, smiling.

Cassie bit her lower lip. Another episode in their new life in Texas pulling her and Bo together. She didn't dare look in Ronny's direction.

"Hey, let's get this show on the road," Tex said. "Let's go in the house. I'm gonna tell you girls what I can do for you with no money and Bo and I are gonna investigate how those two girls got into this place."

CHAPTER 12

"HERE'S WHAT I can do for you," Tex said after taking one look at the bathroom.

Cassie seated herself at the rough kitchen table, ready to hear how Bo's recommended builder could repair their house.

"For fifteen thousand, I can get my plumber in here and work the old plumbing over. After that, I can give you a shiny new bathroom, which will include a new toilet."

"We don't have fifteen thousand dollars to spend on the bathroom," Ronny said. "We don't even know if the whole house is worth that much money."

Cassie remained silent, content to let her sister handle this conversation. Of the two of them, Ronny seemed to be smarter about money.

"But," she added, "we need a new toilet really bad."

"Really bad," Cassie parroted.

"I have to go over to Harlingen to get a commode," Tex said. "I could do that tomorrow. Then I could get my plumber in here day-after-tomorrow to install it. That would cost you four hundred." He raised his hand showing four fingers.

Cassie's eyes bugged. "For a toilet?"

"Ma'am, there's a wide variance in the price of pottys. Four hundred will get you a nice middle-of-the-road fixture. I can get you a cheaper one that you might have to replace next year, but I don't want to leave you girls with something you'll have to repair or replace as soon as I get out the door." He cocked his head and raised his open palms. "It's up to you."

"It's just that we don't have much money," Cassie said meekly.

"I understand. But you've got a toilet that works now, right? You're not having to go outside to go."

"We hate it," Ronny said. "We have to get water out of the sink to make it flush. How much of that four hundred dollars is labor?"

"About half."

"Then you just got yourself a new employee."

Tex raised both palms. "Whoa, whoa, whoa. I'm still thinking about that. I know you want a new toilet now, but it's my opinion that we wait on that 'til we get the plumbing up to date. After that, I can give you the toilet and a nice new fiberglass shower and—"

"We don't like fiberglass," Ronny said. "We want a steel tub. And we want a tile tub surround. Oh, and we want new sinks in the kitchen and bathroom."

Cassie blinked. She didn't know they wanted a steel tub and a tile tub surround. She hadn't had that in the house she rented in Tonawilla and Ronny hadn't had it her apartment either.

"And I wanna marry a rich woman," Tex said. "Darlin', you think I can build a bathroom out of a

Q-Tip? If you want all that, I'm gonna need more money."

"I could do the tile tub surround myself," Ronny said.

"You don't say," Tex said.

"I've done a few. And I can install fixtures if they aren't too complicated."

"You don't say."

"Stop saying that. I told you one of my ex-husbands was a builder."

"What else can you do?"

Not wanting to be left out of the conversation, Cassie piped up. "She can cook pizza in a toaster oven."

Ronny, Tex and Bo looked at her as if she had grown a third head. *Drat!* She had done it again. Said something stupid in front of Bo.

"Tell you what, darlin'—" Tex said to Ronny.

She stopped him. "No, wait. Like my sister said, we don't have a lot of money. We could save money on labor if you hired me as a helper."

Planting his fists on his hips, Tex shook his head. "I've never had a female helper."

"What, you don't like women?"

"Darlin', I love women. Loving women is one of my great failures in life and it's cost me a fortune."

"Well? What does that have to do with me helping with the plumbing?"

"I said I'll think about it. Meanwhile, we'll work out a payment plan."

A direct look came from Ronny to Cassie. "What do you think, Sister?"

"Okay," Cassie said. After a pause, unable to hide her skepticism, she added, "I guess."

"Fine." Tex lifted off his gimme cap and placed it back on his balding head. "I'll get my plumber in here tomorrow to start working on these old pipes."

With the construction work settled more or less, Tex opened his toolbox. "Now, then. Let's check this place out. See if we can figure out how strangers got in."

Cassie and Ronny stayed out of the way while Tex and Bo went through the house. Cassie soon figured out Bo had volunteered to help Tex to save them money. They checked every window and door, installed dead bolts on the front and back doors. After they finished, Tex announced the house was now safe and he prepared to leave.

"So are you going to hire me?" Ronny asked him.

Sometimes Ronny's audacity floored Cassie.

"I'm still thinking about it," Tex said. "We'll be over tomorrow to start on the old pipes. I'll let you know then."

Bo, too, readied to leave. "When do you want to start your classes?" he asked Cassie.

"Monday," she answered promptly. "I need to get my things together. Believe it or not, I brought the books I'll need with me. I suspected from the beginning that I would at least finish out the year in the Tonawilla school."

"Will you need supplies?"

"Uh, well…yes, a few. I don't suppose the little store in town will have any."

"You're right. I'm going over to Harlingen anyway. I'll be glad to take you shopping."

"Really? Oh, my gosh, thank you. I thought I was going to have to drive the taco truck."

As soon as Bo closed the door behind himself, Ronny confronted Cassie. "Thank God he offered to take us to Harlingen. While you shop for school supplies, I can shop for groceries."

But he didn't offer to take us, Cassie griped mentally. He had offered to take *her,* Cassie. "Yeah," she said glumly.

"What's wrong? You look like your dog died."

"Nothing. It's just that—"

"Wait a minute. You're upset because I'm going along. You wanted to spend that alone time with Bo. Look at you." Rubbing her forefingers together, she added in a sing-song voice, like she used to do when they were little kids. "Nah-nah-nah-nah-nah-nah. Going shopping with Bo. Wait until I tell Frank."

"Just stop it, Ronny. He's doing me a favor. Would you want to drive the taco truck with that music playing in Harlingen?"

"All I can say is if we don't figure out a way to alter that damn thing, one of is going to have to learn to make tacos and tamales. And speaking of Frank, have you talked to him yet?"

"How could I talk to him? We don't have phone service worth squat. And it looks like we won't until Tex can put in a pole."

"Get on top of that table outside under the palm trees. I told you, you have to get on top of something to get a good signal. If you don't talk to him pretty soon, he's going to show up down here. He thinks he owns you and he's going to think he needs to check on what you're doing."

"No, he won't. Frank would never make a trip to Texas."

"Oh, yeah?"

Two hours later, Bo was at home in his kitchen heating up his supper when his supervisor Pete McPherson called. "Got any new information?"

"Naw," Bo answered, turning off the burner under a skillet. "We struck out. The builder I told you about thinks, and I tend to agree with him, that Cassie and Ronny left a door unlocked."

"Those girls we picked up told DHS they got in through the fireplace. Of course, neither one of them is coherent. I don't know how credible they are. They barely speak English. They were born in Russia. They've been given drugs and traumatized badly. They've been forced to use so many names they don't even know the names they were given at birth. I don't suppose we could just go in there and arbitrarily tear out that fireplace."

Bo winced. "That would destroy practically that whole wall. I don't know if the sisters will sit still for that."

"They have to. This is as close as we've ever gotten to figuring out what John Jennings was up to. We might even find out who he was working with on the Mexican side. If we have to, we'll try to get subpoenas."

"On what grounds? Cassie and Ronny Jennings haven't done anything wrong."

"I'll figure it out. Don't get excited yet. This is all

new information and we're still analyzing it. I'll be back in touch."

"Okay," Bo said. "And thanks."

He disconnected, his thoughts crashing into each other. If they destroyed the fireplace altogether, half of one side of the house would be open to the outside and the sisters would have no place to live. He was reasonably certain Ronny Jennings would agree to tear down the whole house and go back to New York, but he wasn't so sure about Cassie.

Cassie Jennings appeared to want to make the place a home, even though it clearly wasn't.

He needed to discuss the situation with Tex.

CHAPTER 13

ON MONDAY, AS Cassie prepared to take her teaching job to Bo's house, Ronny went to work for Tex. Though Tex lived in Los Tropicos, most of his work was in Harlingen. He would be picking Ronny up every morning and bringing her home. And for a day or two a week, they would work on their own bathroom.

Time was inching toward the end of January. The weather was balmy and pleasant, even warm. Cassie loved it. She suspected Ronny did, too, though she wouldn't admit it. What was not to love about sitting in sunshine and being able to go about in summer-weight clothing? Back in Tonawilla, people were still shoveling snow.

Aware of the time difference between Texas and New York, Bo picked Cassie up at 6:30 a.m. so she could be prepared to start her online classes at 8:00 east coast time—as if it were his responsibility.

"You don't need to do this," she told him. "Ronny can drive me to your house in the taco truck."

"But you don't like that thing and I don't blame

you. Besides that, it's a shame to shatter the morning calm with that loud music."

They came to a stop in a driveway in front of an unusual carport with an arched opening. "I've never seen a car port like this," Cassie said.

"It's made out of adobe. I figure this house must have been built in the thirties. This is the way they did it back then. Vehicles were smaller. My truck won't fit in it."

"Your yard is beautiful," Cassie said. "Do you keep it up yourself?"

"I have a man who comes by and works on it every week. I like for it to look pretty. In the first place, I don't have a green thumb and in the second, I'm gone a lot. I'd never get it done. I don't have much of a front yard, but the back yard is real nice. I've got an outdoor kitchen."

The first thing she had noticed inside Bo's house was how pleasant it was, though it was old. Like her and Ronny's house, it was a Spanish structure with walls of tan adobe and rust-red tiles on the floor. He jokingly called it his "*adobe hacienda.*" The kitchen and bathrooms had been updated, which gave her a vision of what the house she and Ronny had inherited could be.

His furniture was big like him, and comfortable, and suited the house. The leather upholstery exuded a scent Cassie liked. A decorator from the furniture store where he bought it had put it all together he told her.

He showed her to a massive table in his dining room from which to conduct her lessons. His Internet worked fine and she got off to a roaring start.

When she informed her fifth-graders she was speaking to them from Texas, they were excited and wanted to know all about cowboys and horses.

Every day, she rushed through getting dressed and gulping down a breakfast of a lunchmeat sandwich. At least, they now had sliced bread instead of tortillas.

Most of the time, Bo was out of the house, either doing some chore outside or away from the house altogether, so she conducted her classes without interruption or intrusion. When Bo left the house, he was armed with a pistol attached to his belt. Cassie was growing accustomed to seeing men wearing guns.

If he was inside, he spent more than half his time on the phone in his home office. She still didn't understand what he did for a living.

The beginning of the second week of school, Bo was at home during lunchtime and the aroma of cooking bacon drifted to the dining room. He stuck his head into the dining room. "How about a bacon and tomato sandwich?"

Cassie's diet had been less than even good since they had arrived. She and Ronny had been surviving on lunchmeat sandwiches. With no desire to handwash pots and pans, or wash dishes in general, neither of them cooked.

"That sounds great. Are we having it brought in or are we going somewhere for lunch?"

He grinned. "Making the sandwiches myself."

"Ah. That explains the smell of bacon."

"Mayonnaise okay?"

"That's great," she answered. "I can hardly wait."

Putting together a bacon and tomato sandwich

didn't require great culinary skill, but he had to cook the bacon. He seemed so proud of himself. She scooted onto a tall stool on one side of the cooking island in the middle of his kitchen and watched as he built thick sandwiches of bacon, tomato slices, cheese and crispy lettuce on some kind of rustic bread.

"Oh, my goodness, I don't know if I can get my mouth around that."

"Sure you can," he said, smiling, and poured them two glasses of sweet tea.

She knew sweet tea was a Southern thing, so she made no comment.

As they ate, they talked. "I have to tell you again I really appreciate your letting me come over here and use your Internet. My sister and I desperately need the income from my teaching job."

"If John wanted you to stay here, I don't know why he didn't leave you more money. He certainly knew how few opportunities for work there are in Los Tropicos."

"So you know about the will?"

Chewing, Bo nodded.

"And he money he left us?"

"He told me he was leaving you twenty thousand dollars to fix up the house. He thought if you wanted to stay, you'd figure out how to pay your living expenses."

"Maybe that's all he had."

Bo's head shook. "I don't think so. He was well off."

"Really? Hmm. Well, I assume he didn't get to be *well off* selling tacos and tamales."

"Nobody knows exactly how John made his money. He didn't talk about it. He was a private guy. A lot of people were suspicious that he did something illegal.

"Mr. Thompson at the grocery store implied to my sister that he sold drugs and smuggled people across the border. You knew him. Were you suspicious?"

"At times. But most of the time, he was just a friendly, down-to-earth dude. A good neighbor. I just always figured he played the stock market or something like that." Or maybe he did something in the oil business."

"Oil? Like you pump out of the ground?"

Bo nodded.

"I've read about the oil business in Texas where everyone gets rich. I didn't know it was in this part of the state."

"There's a small amount of activity. Nothing like in West Texas and East Texas. Or even in the Gulf Coast. Still, there's enough going on for people to speculate."

"I hope it's true that he made money legally and honestly. I don't want to think of my father being a criminal. You said you think he had more than twenty thousand dollars. What did he do with the rest of his money? Did he give it to that charity for animals?"

Bo shrugged. "Don't know. I just know he didn't owe any money and the place he left you was debt-free."

"Gosh, I wish Ronny and I had known him. He abandoned us and our mother when we were little kids. They never got a divorce. We've never known why he left or why they stayed married. Since he came to New York from Texas, we don't even know why he was in Tonawilla in the first place.

"Mom passed away in a car accident without telling

us much. We tried to locate him to tell him, but we couldn't find him. Ronny hates him, but I would like to understand him. I don't like hating people."

"I can't shed light on John's past. I only knew him the last couple of years, after I bought this place."

"It's odd that we lived all of our lives without seeing or hearing from him. He never gave us anything, then all of a sudden, he leaves us this land and the house and says we have to live here for a year. Yet he expected us to find jobs to support ourselves.

"We might not be able to stay here whether we want to or not. After school's out, I'll no longer have a teaching job, thus no paycheck. There's nothing for either my sister or me to do in this little town. She got married instead of going to college, so the only thing she's ever done is work in retail in a small town and she was a bartender."

"True, there's not much in Los Tropicos," Bo replied. "If you still want to teach, you'll have to try to get on with the Harlingen school. And that's forty-five miles away."

Forty-five miles notwithstanding, Cassie's thoughts veered to what she would have to do to get a teaching certificate in Texas. If she could possibly prevent it, she had no intention of giving up eighty acres and going back to Tonawilla.

"Ronny really wants to work for Tex. Maye he'll hire her permanently."

After the lunch, they talked more. They even began preparing lunches together every day that he was home. He often cooked something on the grill outside. On those days, lunch became the highlight of her day. He was nothing like Frank. He was quiet and sort of shy. He actually seemed to admire her. He didn't criticize or try to tell her what to do.

She found herself being more drawn to him and having thoughts of being close to him. She scolded herself. She had no business having those thoughts and being unfaithful to Frank. Besides that, in ten more months, she might be back in Tonawilla or Frank might be here if he wanted to be with her.

Soon, the day arrived when Bo came home and told that he and Tex had put up the pole for a satellite dish. "Oh, my gosh," she said ruefully. "That means I'll have to teach my class from my own home."

"It'll take you a few days to get the dish company to come out here. They have to come from Harlingen. You don't have to be in a hurry."

The dish installation took place on a Friday, the week of Valentine's Day. Cassie glumly removed her laptop and her supplies from Bo's roomy dining room. Before he drove her home, he presented her with a single red rose in a pretty little white vase and kissed her cheek. Cassie nearly melted.

"Thank you so much. I forgot it was Valentine's Day," she told him. "I don't have anything for you."

"No matter. I'm just letting you know I've enjoyed your company."

Back home, without smiling, she spread her teaching supplies out on the rustic kitchen table.

"If leaving Bo's house put you in such a bad mood,

why didn't you just continue over there?" Ronny asked. "It isn't that long until school's out."

"I couldn't do that. It's too much of an imposition."

Ronny examined the rose Bo had given her. "I notice you haven't gotten a Valentine's Day gift or even a card from your Tonawilla Romeo. Now, we've got decent phone service. You should call him and give the fool a chance to wish you a happy Valentine's Day."

"You don't like Frank. Why are you so eager for me to call him?"

"Because if you don't, we're going to wake up some morning and he's going to be parked on our doorstep."

Was that possible? Would Frank Kowalski really fly to Texas to see her? "Okay, I'll call him."

"When you do, don't invite him to come here."

"It wouldn't matter if I did. Believe me, Frank Kowalski isn't coming to Texas,

"You hope," Ronny quipped.

"So, Tex's plumber must be getting finished with the pipes. When is he going to finish our bathroom?"

"Soon."

"What are you doing for him in Harlingen?"

"Mostly installing tile backsplashes and sometimes laying tile on floors. And painting. Tex has a lot of houses under construction. I never told you, but after I got a divorce from Tommy Argyle, I thought about starting a company where I laid tile and did painting. He would have hired me. Just because we got divorced didn't mean he didn't realize I did good work."

"You should have done that, Sister."

"Nah. I was too scared and I didn't have the money to buy tools and equipment. Besides, you know me. I'm irresponsible."

"Mike Duffy must not think so. He left you alone in his bar most of the time."

"That's scary, too. By the way, Tex knows the guy who put the big taco on top of the taco truck. And he could take it off. Tex said he doesn't speak much English, so he offered to go with us to ask him to remove it."

"When?"

"Tex said we could go tomorrow. And now that we've got the satellite dish, we can watch TV. Maybe we could get a small TV set."

CHAPTER 14

THE NEXT MORNING, they left home early, with Cassie and Ronny in the taco truck and Tex following. At sixty miles an hour, with "El Rancho Grande" blasting to the heavens, Cassie and Ronny both wore earplugs. Hearing being difficult, they talked little.

It was still early when they arrived in Harlingen at a small white house in need of paint, behind a tall wrought-iron fence. A wide sign in old-world lettering splashed a name all across a steel gate: *Manolo Gaitan Esposito's Grandes y Hermosas Creaciones.*

"Wha-a-a-t?" Ronny said, her brow scrunched into a frown. "What does that say?"

"Something about good creations," Cassie answered.

Metal sculptures of all sizes and shapes littered the front yard. Behind the house and on one side was a sea of wrecked cars and trucks in various stages of dismantlement.

Tex stepped down from his pickup and walked back to where they had parked behind him. "You girls get out."

Cassie cautiously scooted out of the taco truck. Ronny did, too.

"Where are we?" Ronny asked, her hands fisted on her hips. "Is this a junkyard? What does that sign say?"

"Manolo Gaitan Esposito's Grand and Beautiful Creations," Tex supplied.

"Humph, I'll bet," Ronny said, crossing her arms over her chest. "We've already got a taste of his grand creations."

"Manny's a welder," Tex said.

"People pay big bucks for one of his sculptures. He considers himself an artist. Don't hurt his feelings."

"We wouldn't dream of it," Cassie put in. "We need his help."

Just then, a small Mexican man came out of the house. He wore a bright yellow and green Hawaiian shirt and a red bandana tied around his head. His black hair stuck up in a dozen directions. He greeted Tex with open arms and a wide grin. "*Hola! Senor* Barton." In a rapid exchange of Spanish and hand gestures, Tex and he conversed.

Tex directed him over to where Cassie and Ronny stood and introduced them. The Mexican man gestured toward the taco on top of the truck, his brow tented. "John Jennings he like. You no like?"

Cassie answered in a mix of English and limited Spanish. "We don't mean to hurt your feelings, but it doesn't work for us. We don't sell tacos or tamales."

"Is a t'ing of buuu-tee. Everyone love. If I cut off, you no stand out."

"That's kind of what we hope for," Cassie said.

He turned to Tex. "You want? Is *obra de arte*. Will

be buu-tee-ful on top your big truck. I can do. No take long."

"Uh, no thanks, Manny." Tex raised his hands, showing both palms. "All I do with tacos and tamales is eat 'em."

"How much would you charge us to remove it?" Ronny asked.

His deep brown eyes sparking with anger, Manny snapped in English, "You no want sculpture? I keep. You no pay."

Ronny turned to Tex, "Is he saying he'll keep the taco sculpture in exchange for payment to remove it?"

"Yep."

"Sold!" Ronny said.

Manolo dusted his palms together. And threw up his hands. "Okay. I no like to do, but I do. You come back. *Después del almuerzo.*

"What did he say?"

"Come back after lunch," Tex repeated.

They motored away in Tex's luxurious pickup. He took them to a delicious lunch of fine Mexican food. They took their time with lunch, giving Manny plenty of time to remove the taco from the top of the taco truck.

"I'm stuffed," Cassie said. "I didn't know Mexican food could be so good. All I've ever eaten are the tacos Ronny made in Duffy's Tavern."

"Let's get back to Manny's place and get this wrapped up," Tex said. "You girls need a vehicle."

As they neared the welder's house again, Ronny spotted the metallic blue truck even before they

reached the wrought-iron gate. "I see it....OhmyGod!
Oh, my God! Oh. My. God!"

Alarmed, Cassie asked, "What's wrong?"

"Oh! My! God! Is that plywood on top?"

Tex began to laugh. Ronny slugged his shoulder.
"It isn't funny. What if it was *your* truck? And your
only means of transportation in a wasteland?"

Then Cassie spotted it. Her eyes bugged. She
slapped both palms against her cheeks. "Oh, my
goodness!"

Tex pulled to a stop behind the taco truck, which
was now a convertible with a red plywood top. The
windows and windshield remained. "Let's take a
look."

They stepped out of Tex's pickup and walked
around the taco truck, studying it. Some kind of
hanging fringe with little yellow balls adorned the
edge of the red plywood top.

Frowning, Tex rubbed his chin with his thumb and
fingers, as if deep in thought.

"I don't know what to say," Cassie mumbled. "It
looks like he cut the whole top off."

"Shit!" Ronny proclaimed.

Manny came out from inside the house. "You like?
I paint red. Match the blue. *Bonita!*" He kissed his
fingertips.

Before Ronny could put her foot in her mouth,
Cassie spoke up. "It's, uh, unusual."

"My wife, she see new top, say it need somet'ing
else." He placed a hand on the plywood and gave
it a good shake. "*Muy seguro. Construyo con pernos y
tornillos.*"

"What did he say?" Ronny asked.

"He says it's very safe," Tex answered. "He built it with bolts and screws."

"Oh, my God!" Ronny shrieked. "Did he have to cut the top off?"

Cassie looked at Tex. He was obviously suppressing laughter. "Good job, Manny," he said.

He took Ronny's elbow and guided her to the taco truck's driver's side and urged her inside. "Shut-up," he told her *sotto voce*. "He took it off for free."

"What about the music?" Cassie asked Mr. Esposito. "Did you disconnect it?"

"I no know how," he answered.

Before she could say more, Tex took her elbow and guided her to the taco truck's passenger side. "I'll follow you girls home. Drive careful." He turned, shook hands with Mr. Esposito and climbed into his own pickup.

Ronny cussed all the way home. Words Cassie didn't know her sister knew. She could be heard even above *"El Rancho Grande"* and the wind whistling through the cracks between the windshield, the windows and the plywood top

"You worked in that bar too long. I never heard such language," Cassie told her in a yell. "At least the red color doesn't look bad with the blue pickup."

"Oh, My God! What the hell are we going to do, Cassie?" Ronny threw a hand in the air. "We can't drive around in this piece of shit. Instead of looking like we're selling tacos and tamales, now, we look like hookers driving around playing *"El Rancho Grande"* for attention. My God. People are going to wonder if we have a mattress in back."

"I can't drive around in it anyway," Cassie replied.

"I don't think I'll ever learn to shift gears. Maybe we can remove the fringe."

"With what? A blowtorch? With a good fire, we could remove the whole friggin' top!"

At home, Ronny came to a stop in front of the door into the courtyard and Tex stopped behind them.

"Aren't you going to park in the barn?" Cassie asked her sister.

"No. I'm leaving this piece of shit parked on the road. I hope some fool steals it."

She hit the ground and slammed the door.

"But Ronny—"

"Don't talk to me. I'm going to find that damn airplane ticket. I'm going back to New York." She stomped into the house.

Cassie turned to Tex. "She's upset. Did he have to cut the top off?""

Tex cocked his head and lifted both palms. "Look at it this way. You girls need a vehicle and it runs fine. The red color looks good with the pretty blue metallic."

"Everyone keeps saying that. I just have to learn to drive it."

"I'll put it in the barn for you." Tex climbed into the taco truck, drove it around the house and into the barn. He walked back to where Cassie stood beside his pickup and handed her the taco truck's keys.

"Thank you for doing that and for going with us to Harlingen," she said.

"You're welcome. You think she'll really go back to New York?"

"No. I'm not going back and she wouldn't leave me. She thinks she needs to look out for me."

Tex nodded. "I'd miss her. She's a good hand."

Cassie nodded, too. "Ronny's smart. She can do almost anything....Well, I'd better go inside and peel her off the ceiling."

"Tell her we've got a tile job in Harlingen tomorrow. I'll pick her up at six o'clock."

CHAPTER 15

VALENTINE'S DAY HAD come and gone. Every day, Cassie thought about Bo giving her a rose and kissing her cheek. He had touched her heart.

On Sunday morning, she and her sister sat at the table with cups of coffee

Just having crawled out of bed, Ronny looked like her typical self: raccoon eyes and stale makeup, bed hair that had grown past her waist and still showed red and green streaks left over from the Christmas holidays. Neither of them had found a hairdresser in Los Tropicos.

Add to that, a red-rose tattoo encircled Ronny's left arm, climbing from her wrist to her shoulder. She had gotten it on a dare from someone at Duffy's Tavern. As tattoos went, Cassie had always thought the artwork quite good. In Tonawilla, Ronny had stood out as a rebel who sometimes had made Cassie roll her eyes and shake her head. Here, in Los Tropicos, Texas, there was no one to notice.

Cassie knew she herself looked as she did most mornings: fresh faced and bright eyed, freckles across her nose. She had no tattoo. Though Ronny had tried to talk her into it, she had resisted. As for her naturally curly hair, a quick brush through it was all it took to put it in place.

"I found out there's a little Catholic church in town," Ronny said, examining her fingernails. "Wow, do I need a manicure....We could go to mass. If anyone needs a prayer or two, it's us."

"You haven't been to church since you started working in Duffy's Tavern."

Ronny gathered her hair and pulled the strands around and over her shoulder, combing her fingers through it and inspecting the ends.

"Your hair's getting so long" Cassie said. "And it still has red and green streaks. We're well past Christmas. Maybe you should think about a different color."

"Changing the color calls for a trip to Harlingen." She continued to play with the ends of her hair. "I think I'll go with purple next time. Purple looks good with brown hair." She gathered it into a ponytail and secured it with a scrunchie.

Cassie's own hair had grown out and covered her head in a halo of blond curls and waves. "I can't believe we have to go all the way to Harlingen to get our hair done."

Just then, a light *rap-rap-rap* sounded on the front door. Except for Bo and Tex and a few construction people, no one visited them.

Uh-oh. They must have forgotten to lock the door into the courtyard. Cassie felt a drop in her stomach. Wide-eyed, she looked at Ronny. "Are you expecting someone?"

Ronny glared at the door. "No."

"That Mr. Thompson said we shouldn't open the door to anyone."

"I heard him. What are we supposed to do? Pretend we aren't home?"

"Right. It's silly." Summoning her nerve, Cassie drew a deep breath, got to her feet, strode to the front door and opened it.

Bo stood there, a wide smile on his face, a gleam in his dark chocolate eyes. Her heart trilled with joy, but immediately she rued his seeing her with no makeup.

He, on the other hand, looked as if he just stepped off a magazine cover. Instead of his usual dress shirt, he was wearing a T-shirt with a red, white and blue image. The snug fit showed off his wide shoulders and muscular, tanned arms. Cassie nearly swooned.

"Got coffee?" he asked. "I'll trade you some fresh doughnuts."

Cassie laughed, self-consciously touching her hair. "Of course. Come in. Mr. Thompson said we shouldn't open the door to anyone, so we almost didn't."

Bo walked in, the box of doughnuts balanced on one hand. "When did he say that?"

"A couple of weeks ago when we went to talk to him about Wi-Fi. Ronny told him about coming home and finding the two strange girls in the house."

"Hm," Bo said. "That's interesting." He set the box on the table and opened it. The sweet confection's aroma filled the air.

"Yum. Those smell fresh," Ronny said. "Look good, too." She poured coffee into a thick mug and set it on the table. "Here's a cup of coffee to go with them. Have a seat."

"Bo," Cassie said, grabbing his attention and looking into his eyes. "I meant to talk to you about this before now. That Mr. Thompson said things go on around here that young ladies shouldn't be involved in. Are we in danger?"

A frown formed between Bo's brows. "I don't think so. But it doesn't hurt to be cautious. It's true there's a lot of people-smuggling and drug traffic coming from Mexico."

"That's not something we haven't already heard," Ronny said. "I don't know how we would know if we met one of those."

She helped herself to a chocolate covered doughnut. "Where did you get fresh doughnuts so early in the morning?"

Bo gestured for Cassie to sit, but before she did, she pulled several paper plates and plastic forks from the cupboard and tore off several sheets of paper towel.

After Cassie sat, Bo lifted his cowboy hat off and placed it upside down on the sofa. Cassie had noticed that cowboy hats seemed to require special treatment. Seeing a man wearing a cowboy hat in Tonawilla was like spotting a unicorn, but here, it seemed that most men wore one.

"They had them at the cafe in town," he said. "Clay's wife doesn't make them every day, but when she does, they don't last long. Everybody who goes into the store buys some. I grabbed the last box of a dozen."

With a grin, he picked up a plastic fork, speared a doughnut and dropped it onto a paper plate. "I like the crème-filled ones, but they're messy."

"That Elena Thompson cooks everything, doesn't she?" Ronny bit into a thick doughnut.

"She sure does. And she's a good cook, too. People come from far and wide to eat in that café."

"Thank you so much for thinking of us," Cassie said and daintily placed a doughnut on her paper plate.

Bo smiled. "Glad to have an excuse to come by. I miss you in my dining room."

Cassie had been gone from his dining room only two days. Her cheeks warmed. She beamed a smile at him. "Aww. I miss you, too."

"Alright already," Ronny said. "You two are making me sick. These doughnuts are sweet enough. Stuff one in your mouth and shut up."

Bo's cheeks reddened and he stiffened. Cassie wanted to slap her sister for embarrassing him.

"Get your Wi-fi working okay?" he asked.

"It seems to be. I'll know for sure tomorrow when I start my class."

"Now that we've got it, I want to get a TV," Ronny said. "It would be nice to step back into the civilized world."

Just then, another louder knock sounded on the door.

Cassie and Ronnie exchanged looks. "I'll get it," Ronny said. She left her chair and strode to the door, opened it with a flourish. "Oh, my God! Frank!"

As if he were an apparition, Frank's image was silhouetted in the doorway by the early morning sunlight. Cassie's eyes bugged; her breath caught. "Frank?"

Springing to her feet, she bumped her chair and knocked it over with a bang.

"Who's Frank?" Bo asked.

"Aren't you going to ask me to come in?" Frank Kowalski asked Ronny.

"Uh, sure. Come on in."

With an I-told-you-so glare at Cassie, Ronny swung the door open wide.

Cassie shot Bo a pleading look. But before she could speak, Frank walked in and dropped his duffel on the floor by the door. He marched across the room as if he owned it, leaned and kissed Cassie's cheek. Wearing his elevator shoes, Frank was the same height as she.

"I gotta tell you, honey, I'm surprised you and your sister ever found this place. I almost didn't find it myself."

Cassie's heart was beating like a snare drum. She thought she might faint. Steeling herself by bracing her fingertips on the table, she stammered, "Well, uh, I—"

"Boudreaux McKenzie Buckalew," Bo said, getting to his feet and extending his right hand. He had risen to his full six-feet-two, adding to his height by leveling his wide shoulders. Looking down at Frank, he added, "My friends call me Bo."

Frank shook hands, at the same time eyeing him from head to toe and back again, his gaze landing on the pistol attached to Bo's belt. "My word. I thought the stories I've heard about Texans and guns were a joke."

"I don't know what you've heard," Bo replied affably, "but there's a good chance it's true."

"What I've heard is that this state is the Wild West. Any man, woman or child can carry a weapon. No restrictions, no background check, just the money to purchase."

"You couldn't be more mistaken, Frank, is it? No states are lacking in gun laws, even Texas. And I would add, the word weapon covers a wide spectrum of instruments."

"Is that gun loaded?"

"Sure is," Bo answered with a smile. "No point in carrying it if it's not loaded. I may never use it. Hope I don't, but these days, I'd rather have it if it's needed than be without it. I'm a dead shot. I always hit where I aim."

A silly half-grin tipped up one corner of Frank's mouth. He was obviously nervous. "Sure, sure. I get it. Beauregard is it?"

No one spoke, silence filled the room. Finally, Bo said, "I assume you're from New York. Are you related to Cassie and Ronny?"

Frank looped a possessive arm around Cassie's shoulders and drew her closer. She pushed against him, but he held her firmly in place and she couldn't free herself without causing a commotion.

"Cassie and I are engaged," Frank said, looking at her. "About five years, isn't it, Cass?" He looked up at Bo. "We've known each other most of our lives."

Cassie was embarrassed, mortified and more than a little miffed. She had thought very little about Frank since they arrived in Texas and hearing the word "engaged" brought on a visceral response. She stared at the floor, swallowing hard to keep from throwing up. She felt Bo's eyes boring a hole into the top of her head.

"Engaged?" Bo said. "Well, my goodness, Cassie. You didn't tell me you were engaged. I suppose congratulations are in order."

He walked over to the sofa, picked up his hat and set it on. "Guess I better get back to what I need to be doing." He turned his attention back to Frank. "Pleased to meet you, buddy. Enjoy yourself down here in the Wild West." He looked directly at Cassie, but said, "Ladies, I'll talk to you later."

Frank's eyes followed him across the room and stayed on him until the door closed behind him. He planted his hands on his skinny hips. "Well. Whaddayaknow? A real live cowboy. How did you lasso him?" He gave a stupid heh-heh-heh. "Lasso. Get it?"

Ronny's eyes rolled. "Oh, puu-leeze."

"He's our—our—our neighbor," Cassie stammered, her hands clasped tightly in front of her. "He helps us out sometimes."

"He helps us with our cows," Ronny put in.

Frank's brows climbed up his forehead. "Cows? You've got cows?"

Ronny jammed her fists against her hips again and thrust her face forward. "We sure do."

Cassie stiffened her shoulders defensively. "We have four. They're pets."

"Pet cows? Cassie, are you out of your mind?"

Rarely felt anger began to simmer within Cassie. "Our father left them to us," she snapped.

"*Humph. So* this is your inheritance. This shack and four pet cows." Frank perused the doughnuts.

"Mother told me it wouldn't amount to much. Interesting place though. What's up with that other door? You trying to keep someone out or in?"

"It's old Spanish architecture. It's historical," Ronny snapped.

"Don't denigrate it," Cassie added.

He gave another silly heh–heh–heh and picked up a doughnut with multi-colored sprinkles. "I didn't get breakfast this morning. Got any more of that coffee?"

"The pot's on the counter," Cassie said.

Frank looked around and ambled over to the counter, reached into the cupboard for a mug and poured coffee. As he chomped into the doughnut, a shower of sprinkles landing on the front of his green polo shirt.

"Why didn't you tell me you were coming?" Cassie asked.

"Decided at the last minute," he said, chewing a mouthful of doughnut. "I haven't heard from you, so…." He shrugged and sipped his coffee, then walked into the hallway, toward the bedrooms, leaving a trail of crumbs and sprinkles on the tile floor behind him.

"Bastard. I just mopped that floor," Ronny grumbled in a loud whisper. "I told you, Cassie. Didn't I tell you he'd show up down here?"

Cassie pressed her fingertips against her forehead. "I think I've got a headache."

"I'll say," Ronny quipped. She met Frank coming back from his stroll through the house. "So, uh, Frank, how was your trip?'

"You've got to really want to get to this place. Especially if you're driving a car that's more like a roller skate." He stuffed the last of his doughnut into his mouth and set his empty mug on the table.

"You don't even have to tell me, you're ready to come home. I mean, who in their right mind would stay here? This house might be historical, whatever *that* means, but it's a real piece of shit. Mother agreed that I could buy you a plane ticket home."

The anger that had lay simmering streaked up Cassie's spine. Her hands clenched into fists. "I would, Frank! I would want to stay here! And I'm going to! And you were rude to our friend!"

Frank's face went from pale to red. "Don't tell me it's the cowboy. I would have expected something like a schoolgirl crush from your sister on this fiction hero, but you? You're educated. I thought you were better than that."

Ronnie glowered down at Frank. "Well excuse the hell out of me, Mr. Success. I think I resent that remark. Bo has been a good friend to us since we got here and a perfect gentleman. If I had to pick out a man for Cassie, I wouldn't even think twice about choosing Bo....And he doesn't have a mother."

Frank stepped backward, away from Ronny who was a head taller than he. Her height and brashness had always intimidated him.

He turned to Cassie. "What do you have to say for yourself, Cassie? If I'd known this BS was going on I wouldn't have made this trip. It's taken a lot of my time and the ticket cost me a lot of money."

As if on "automatic," Cassie's face thrust forward until it was only inches from Frank's. "If you had let me know you were coming, I'd have told you not to waste your time or your money. Bo might not be the man in my future, but I can tell you for certain, there's one who won't be."

Cassie strode to the front door and yanked it open. "I'm sorry it took me so long to see through you, Frank. As we say in Texas, don't let the door hit you in the ass."

As he stamped toward the door, Frank let out a string of expletives she'd never heard him say. He stopped in the doorway. "Obviously, you're not the person I thought you were, Cassandra. Don't bother to call when you've come to your senses."

"Go! Home!" Cassie shouted.

"I'm going. Mother was right all along. She'll be happy to know I've dodged a bullet."

Ronny shouted from behind her. "If Bo was here with his gun right now, I guarantee there's a bullet you wouldn't dodge. I'd put one right between your eyes."

"Blah, blah, blah," Frank said. "By the way, Mother thought your old car looked bad parked in her driveway." He yanked a folded piece of paper from his back pocket. "She made a record of the time it's been there. Here's her bill." He flipped the paper to the floor. "I'll be calling the township and telling them she's got an old, abandoned car parked at her house."

"You do that, ass-hat," Ronny snarled, "and I'll be making a special trip back to New York just to set her house on fire."

"What a couple of losers!" Frank yelled, shaking his head. He strode toward his Smart Car.

"Hey, asshole!" Ronny yelled back. "Don't forget this." With a powerful underhanded pitch like the

softball pitcher she had been in high school, she
threw his duffel out the door and into the courtyard.

He stamped back and picked it up. "If you come
to your senses, Cassie, I've got a room in Harlingen
at *El Gato Negro*. If I don't hear from you, I'm going
home tomorrow."

"Good-bye, Frank!"

Still trembling from an adrenaline rush, Cassie
slammed the door and let out a huff, pressing a palm
against her pounding heart. She looked at Ronny.
"Oh, my gosh. I can't believe you threatened to burn
his mother's house down. I can't believe I talked to
him like that."

"You go girl," Ronny said, giving a thumbs up. "I
can't believe he talks to *you* like that, Cassie. You're the
one who's dodged a bullet. He treats you like you're
dumber than he is. You're the one who graduated
from college. He dropped out."

"Be fair, Ronny. He had to. After his dad died, he
had to take care of his mother."

Ronny's head shook. "Bullshit."

"I've never seen him so mad."

"Don't worry about it. Mommy will give him
some cookies and warm milk and he'll be fine."

Still shaking, Cassie sank to a chair at the table,
planted her elbows on the surface and covered her
face with her hands.

"What's *El Gato Negro*?" Ronny asked. "I don't
remember seeing that anywhere."

"Me, neither. It means the black cat."

"No shit? That sounds like a joint that rents rooms
by the hour." The corners of her mouth tipped up in
an evil grin. "Can you see Frank Kowalski in a place

like that? His mother would have a heart attack. She would have to have him fumigated and disinfected before she would let him back in the house."

Out of her control, a laugh blurted from Cassie and she looked at her sister. "A bullet between his eyes? When did you become a sharpshooter?"

"I was afraid you were going to let the damn bully get by with insulting you and me and Bo and everything else."

"Nice to meet you, Annie Oakley. What am I going to do about my car?"

"I'll call Mike Duffy. He's a good friend. He'll pick it up and park it at his house alongside mine."

"We might as well sell those cars if we can. Would Mike Duffy help us do that?"

"Cassie, no. What will we drive when we go back to New York?"

"Ronny, get it through your head. I'm not going back to New York. Even if we did, those cars are old. Yours is already junk."

"We have to go back. We can't make a living here, Cassie."

"Yes, we can. I'm going to get certified to teach in Texas. Maybe we don't stay in Los Tropicos. After a year maybe we can sell this place and move somewhere where I can teach. Texas is a big place. We'll figure out something for you to do. But for the moment, I need to go to Bo's house. I need to explain."

"Right now?"

"Yes, right now while my nerve is up."

"I was planning for us to go to town today, do a

little shopping in the grocery store and wash a load of clothes."

"Ronny, please. I really need to talk to Bo and I don't know if I can drive the taco truck. Even if I could, I wouldn't leave you here alone."

"Okay, how about this? I'll drop you off at Bo's, go to town and do the chores, then pick you up when I'm finished."

Cassie couldn't keep from grinning with relief. "That'll work. Thank you, thank you, thank you."

CHAPTER 16

CASSIE AND RONNY made themselves presentable. The last thing Cassie wanted was for Bo to see her the way she looked earlier when he dropped by with the doughnuts.

As they drove toward his house, Cassie asked, "Is it my imagination or didn't we just buy groceries?"

"I know," Ronny replied. "Maybe we're eating in our sleep."

"We've been gone a lot lately. Do you suppose someone has come in the house and taken food?"

"Not unless we've got ghosts. Tex and Bo fixed the windows and doors. And we've been careful to lock everything."

"It just seems like we're buying a lot of groceries."

They arrived at Bo's house and found Bo in his barn, brushing one of his horses.

Cassie scooted out of the taco truck and waved Ronny away. She walked over to the corral and peeked over the top fence rail. "Hi. You probably heard me coming."

Bo smiled. "Can't miss that loud mariachi music. You sure can't sneak up on anybody."

Reins in his hand, he led the horse over to where she stood, watching the taco truck disappear into the horizon. "Where's your sister off to?"

"To town to get some things at the store and do a load of laundry. Don't worry. She's coming back to get me. You aren't stuck with me. I just wanted to talk to you a minute about Frank."

"I wasn't worried. I'd never consider your presence being *stuck* with you. Frank leave?"

"He's going back to New York. I'll probably never see him again."

"You broke up?"

"There wasn't much to break up. He was never really my fiancé. He was just sort of a boyfriend."

Bo nodded. "I see."

"I hope you aren't mad at me."

"Not mad exactly. Just kind of disappointed. You weren't honest with me."

Inside, she winced. She never, ever wanted to disappoint him. Tears burned behind her eyes, but reminded that Ronny called her a crybaby, she swallowed them back. "I know I should have told you about him. It's just that I didn't know what to do. I've hardly thought about him since we've been here. Who I've thought about is you. I've never met anyone like you. You're like someone I might read about in a book."

"That's flattering, Cassie, but I'm just a plain-vanilla guy. My sisters would tell you I'm a dull clod. I pride myself in being honest in my relationships with people. I like for other people to do the same."

He removed the reins from the horse, slapped it on the rump and it trotted away to be with two other horses. "You know how to ride?" he asked her.

She couldn't prevent the laugh that blurted out. "Hardly. This is as close as I've ever been to a horse. I thought they'd be scary, but they seem almost gentle."

"These *are* gentle. They're good-natured. Seasoned pleasure horses. I don't need three, but I like them."

"They're really big, aren't they?"

He chuckled. "I weigh two hundred pounds. I need a big mount."

"Is that how you decide the right size? You match your size to the size of the horse? I would probably need a hobbyhorse."

He chuckled again. "You're funny." He opened the corral gate, walked through and came over to her. "I could trade one of these for a smaller horse. Then I'd teach you to ride."

Hearing that he wasn't mad lifted her heart. "Really? Oh, my gosh. That would be wonderful. I've got cowboy boots, you know."

"I remember when you bought them." He took her elbow and urged her toward the house. "We'll have to get you a saddle next time we go to Harlingen. Let's go to the house. Have some lunch and a glass of tea and you tell me about Frank."

Sitting at the cooking island in Bo's cheery kitchen with a ham and cheese sandwich and a glass of iced sweet tea, Cassie explained her relationship with Frank Kowalski. At the end of it, she said, "He never gave me a ring or anything like that. We never really made a plan to get married. It was just something he assumed and the people around town expected."

"Expected?"

"Tonawilla is a small town. Smaller than Harlingen

and isolated by the mountains. Everyone knows everyone and they are all minding each other's business. Frank is considered a success. A good catch. I sort of went along because people wanted me to and because it seemed like I had no other choice.

"I used to admire him, but I guess I grew up. Now, he gets on my nerves and my sister can't stand him. If they're in the same room together, it's like a bunch of firecrackers might go off all at once."

"I sensed the friction."

She looked deeply into his beautiful brown eyes. "He's—he's not like you."

Bo reached across the island and took her hands, rubbed the tops with his thumbs. "I'm glad I got to meet Frank. He doesn't deserve a sweet, beautiful woman like you. We're more than friends, Cassie. I think about you all the time. It was great having you here in my dining room every day. I meant it when I said I miss you."

Cassie almost cried from pure joy. "Oh, Bo, me, too."

He smiled. "I never dreamed I'd fall for a Yankee girl."

She returned his smile. "And I never dreamed I'd even meet, much less fall for a long, tall Texan."

He continued to rub the back of her hands with his thumbs. "I've got to go to Austin to talk to my boss, but I'll be back in a few days. I'll call you as soon as I get back."

"Is that far from here?"

"Three hundred miles or so."

"Oh. That's a long drive. Back home, that would take me across three states." She tittered nervously.

"I'm flying. Driving takes too much time. I told Tex I was gonna be gone. He's agreed to feed the cows."

"We'll be fine. Ronny and I need to learn to do that. There's no reason we should be depending on other people to do things we can do for ourselves. They're steers, right. Should we be calling them cows?"

"Cows is a generic term applied to all cattle, male or female. I don't mind feeding them. Longhorns are a part of Texas culture. Also, a part of history. I like 'em. Those four are so docile, they're like big dogs."

"Well, their food is higher than dog food."

"You've still got a good supply of hay in the barn. When you get low, we'll figure something out."

"That'll be great." She began to gather their dishes. "Thanks for the sandwich. Your ham sandwiches are better than ours. Ours don't have cheese or lettuce and tomatoes." She got to her feet and picked up the stack of dishes. "It's nice to eat on dishes instead of paper plates. I don't mind the paper plates, but still..." She shrugged.

She carried the plates and silverware to the sink and turned on the faucet. He followed with the glasses.

"Do you have to go?" he asked, setting the glasses in the sink.

His arm looped around her shoulders. He was close enough that his body touched hers. Her heart began to pound. She turned off the faucet and looked up into his face, found his dark eyes even darker, his expression serious. "I don't...don't have to do anything I don't want to."

"I could take you home later," he said softly. His

head bent and he kissed her, a real all-out kiss filled
with passion. She didn't even consider not kissing
him back. It seemed to go on forever and left her
dizzy.

"Damn, Cassie," he murmured.

Silence surrounded them. They were totally alone
in a cocoon of intimacy as she had never known it.

"Bo, I—"

"My bedroom's about twenty steps away."

"Oh? I've never been in your bedroom."

"I know."

"I, uh…I could call Ronny and tell her not to
come get me."

"About time you got home," Ronny said. "You've
been gone all day. Don't tell me you and Bo have
been doing the nasty."

Cassie was too happy to let her sister's needling
rattle her. She turned in a circle around the room.
"Oh, Ronny, he's the most wonderful man I've ever
known."

"That good, huh?"

"Oh, Ronny, he told me he never dreamed he'd fall
for a Yankee girl."

"I told you he was smitten. Wonder how many
Yankee girls he's ever met."

"It almost feels like we're planning a future
together."

"So, now what?"

"He's going to Austin for a few days to meet with

his boss. I don't know who his boss is and I still don't know what company he works for. I meant to ask him, but I didn't think about it."

"He's got a weird job alright. He doesn't have regular hours and he seems to have a lot of freedom away from work. Austin's the capitol. Maybe he works for the government. Or maybe he's a traveling salesman of some kind."

"He arranged with Tex to help us with the cows while he's gone."

"That's good. I like the cows, but I hate going out in that pasture. A big snake could be lurking just waiting for me."

"Mr. Atwater said snakes will run from you."

"I don't want to test that idea. Do you?"

"Of course not."

"I've got some news, too," Ronny said. "I've been dying for you to get home so I could tell you. Clay and Elena hired me to help Elena in the kitchen on weekends and work in the store if Clay needs to be away for some reason."

"Oh, my gosh. Really? How did that happen?"

"The store and café weren't busy today, so Clay and Elena and I got a chance to visit. They're really friendly, you know. I told them about my experience working at Dollar General. I told them I had done every job in that store from cleaning the toilets to merchandising and managing the money. Even making hotdogs."

"I can't imagine how that store manager has been getting along since you left. He probably has had to actually show up in the store."

"And I told them about tending bar," Ronny

went on. "That's when they asked me if I wanted a weekend job working in the cafe."

"That's great....But you can't cook. You're going to be a waitress?"

"They don't have waitresses. Customers order food at the counter. The girls in the kitchen will take it out to them if they're at a table. I'm going to be Elena's assistant. In other words, the grunt. But she's going to teach me to cook Mexican food. I learned to make pizza in Duffy's Tavern and hotdogs in Dollar General, so surely I can learn to make Mexican food."

Cassie gave a huff. "You didn't *make* pizza. It came frozen. I'm not sure you have to be a cook to make hotdogs."

"So?" Ronny's shoulders lifted in a shrug and she showed her palms. "Small difference. I made tacos from scratch, though. Hell, you know me. I can do anything I set my mind to. You know that fancy Mexican restaurant Tex took us to in Harlingen? Elena cooked there for years before she met Clay. Both of her parents worked there, too. Her parents have been working in Mexican food restaurants forever and she grew up in a restaurant kitchen."

"No wonder she's such a good cook."

"That's why people drive over here all the way from Harlingen to eat. They know her and the kind of food she cooks. The recipes are her own that she made up. She's an interesting woman. She was born in Mexico, but her parents brought her here when she was four years old."

"Are they illegals?"

"Her parents are and they make no secret of it. They've lived in Harlingen over forty years. It's weird down here, the way people seem to wander back and forth across the border."

"If her parents are illegal, what does that make Elena?"

"I don't know. She went all through school in Harlingen. Even went to the community college in Harlingen a couple of years. She speaks almost perfect English. It's still her second language though. She lapses into Spanish sometimes."

"Is she in danger of being deported?"

"She isn't worried about it. She says people like her and her parents are of low interest to ICE."

"I don't know what that means, but what are you going to do about helping Tex?"

"I'll still do tile work for him. That's a hit-or-miss situation. He doesn't always need me and he doesn't work on weekends anyway. The weekend job at the café will be steady. I'm also going to help Clay re-do some things in the store. That store needs some work. I learned a lot about retail all the years I worked at Dollar General."

"All of that is good news, Sister. With both of us employed, we'll make it."

"I'm not finished. That's not the best news. Clay and Elena want to sell the store and café so they can travel. Elena has never been out of Texas. They want to get a motor home and travel around the US. They want to work on her getting legal citizenship so they don't run into any problems. He asked me if I would be interested in buying them out."

Cassie's breath caught. She could see excitement bubbling in her sister, enthusiasm she hadn't seen in her in a very long time.

"Oh, my gosh, Ronny. But you don't have any money and I don't either. What did you tell them?"

"I told them I'd let them know. I've been thinking about something."

"I'm almost afraid to ask."

"Do you suppose Tex would front me in buying that store and café?"

Cassie's eyes widened. "I don't know. He seems to have plenty of money. And he seems to trust you."

"I can't think of any other place to get money. I'm going to ask him."

CHAPTER 17

THAT NIGHT, RONNY went to bed early, but she lay awake tossing and turning, her mind filled with future plans. She had always been the one who endorsed the back of a check, never signed the front. For that matter, until she and Cassie set up checking and savings accounts in Harlingen, she had never had a bank account.

In every job she had ever held—which, in Tonawilla, New York, were few—eventually she had been promoted to running the operation. Though she was a part-time employee in Duffy's Tavern, Mike Duffy had started leaving her in charge on the busiest nights of the week, Fridays and Saturdays.

During the years she had worked at Dollar General, half a dozen managers had come and gone, either because they had been fired or moved on to other stores. Between their tenures, she had temporarily managed the store. She had often thought she could do a better job as the official manager, but, at the end of the day, she had walked away from the pressure and responsibilities of being *the boss*. She left money on the table that could have been hers.

The possibility of a role reversal was terrifying, but still exhilarating as nothing else had ever been.

Oddly enough, approaching Tex didn't concern her at all. They had developed a bond of trust. He was a smart businessman. He would recognize the value of the café and store to the town of *Lost* Tropicos and the potential for higher revenue a good manager could bring.

If she feared anything, she feared he might buy it out from under her. She trusted him, but—well, you just never knew about people one hundred percent. All the more reason to approach him early, before Clay presented him with the opportunity.

With that decision made, fatigue overtook her and she fell into a deep and peaceful sleep.

She rose bright and early the next morning. Tex would soon pick her up for a trip to Harlingen to do a tile job. She closed Cassie's bedroom door so as not to wake her. Last night, both of them had been exhausted when they called it a night.

As coffee brewed, she checked out the box of doughnuts Bo had brought yesterday. To her surprise, only two doughnuts were left in the box. She did a quick inventory. Bo had brought a dozen doughnuts. She, Cassie, Bo and Idiot Frank had each eaten one, leaving eight. Someone had eaten six.

Damn, I'll have to keep an eye on Cassie. She shouldn't be eating this much calorie-filled stuff.

Just as she returned to the counter for a coffee refill, she recognized the clatter of Tex's monster truck pulling to a stop outside. Her pulse picked up. "This is it," she mumbled. "No pain, no gain."

Before he could knock, she opened the door and greeted him with a big smile. "I was going to call you as soon as I got up but I thought it was too early."

"Darlin' you can't call too early for me. Sleep is a waste of time. What's up? You're grinning like a cat that found a shitload of catnip."

Ronny laughed. She might never get accustomed to the colorful greetings her new friend came up with. "What are you doing here so early?"

"Tile job in Harlingen, remember?"

"Of course I remember." She filled a to-go cup with coffee and grabbed her purse. "Okay, let's go."

The minute they hit the road headed north, she jumped right in. She told him about Clay and Elena hiring her to work in the store and the cafe, then talking to her about buying them out. She even threw in a couple of her own ideas to upgrade the store.

Tex drove like a race car driver, so she talked rapidly so she could get everything said before the drive from *Lost* Tropicos to Harlingen ended.

"I could add another washing machine and dryer so washing and drying clothes wouldn't take all day. In this town, you've got a captured stream of customers with nothing better to do than watch the dryer spin their clothes. Women like to browse. I could put in jewelry, hair accessories, even makeup. Inexpensive items that are impulse buys.

"And after a while, I might even set up a station for a hairdresser. The way things are now, you have to drive all the way to Harlingen to get your hair done."

"Hold on, girl," Tex replied. "You're gonna hurt something if you keep talking at this speed. I'm taking a wild guess here, but you must be telling me this because somehow, I figure into your plans."

"I want you to go into business with me."

Tex never drove slower than eighty. He didn't take his eyes off the road, nor did he slow down. "Let's step back a minute. What's Clay asking for the place? Did you look at his books? I believe he turns a profit, but there could be hidden expenses. How soon does he want to do this?"

Ronny's shoulders fell. Those were very good questions and she hadn't thought to ask any of them. "I never really got that far."

"When you say 'go into business with me,' that's a hint to me that you'll be putting in funds. I thought you were broke."

"Well….Well, technically I am."

"So, what you really want is for me to front the purchase. Any thoughts on how I'd get repaid?"

Ronny felt uneasy, if there was anything in life she was good at, it was reading men and playing into their ego. Until Tex, she had never met her match, but instinct told her he was deliberately dragging this out, having fun with her inexperience and naïveté. She played along, hoping for a good outcome.

"Did I mention the new merchandise that could be brought into the store? The women in town can't even buy a tube of lipstick. The store doesn't have—"

"Darlin', I'm gonna put you out of your misery, though teasing you and listening to you is kinda fun. Clay talked to me about buying that business long before you and your sister ever showed up in Los Tropicos."

Ronny slugged his shoulder. "Asshole. You could have told me that earlier and saved me the cheerleader bullshit."

Tex grinned. "I was hoping the pompons were going to be pulled out. Or at the very least, I'd see a cartwheel."

"Get out," Ronny grouched, set her jaw and crossed her arms over her chest. "I'm embarrassed."

"Oh, come on now. We need to talk about this some more. I already gave some thought to you helping me out with this idea I've got. I mean, you're wasting your talent installing tile."

Ronny's enthusiasm inched back. "What's your idea."

"It's like this. I know that old building. I already remodeled the apartment where Clay and Elena live and he's talked to me before about updating the rest of it. There's a good-sized space that butts up to the kitchen. He and Elena use it to store junk. I picture making that space a bar. I'd cut a hole in the café wall and make an access to the café. Customers in the bar could get tacos and enchiladas out of the café if they wanted to.

"I'd dress up that parking lot in the back. Put in good lighting and security cameras. I'd put a door back there for customers coming into the bar. That way, shoppers in the store wouldn't be distracted by the bar traffic."

"Holy cow. You'd serve booze?"

"Just beer and wine."

"I told you I used to be a bar tender, didn't I? I've got a license in New York."

"That doesn't do us much good in Texas. Let me

finish. I'd add a couple of big screen TVs. A lot of people in Los Tropicos can't get TV, can't ever get the big sports events. I'd add two or three comfortable chairs, maybe a couple of little tables, and have a little sports bar. 'Course I'd put in new lighting and bring everything up to code."

Ronny was excited again. "There's a code in *Lost Tropicos?*"

"There's a code in Harlingen. That's what I'd go by. Having things up to code is a good idea, especially with electrical and plumbing."

Obviously, he had given this a lot of thought. "But you'd own everything. I'd be just an employee."

"Nope. I'll just own the building and the bar. You'll buy the restaurant and equipment and the inventory on a contract with me. You'll pay me an agreed-on amount monthly and in turn for your help in the bar, I'll give you a percentage of the bar revenue."

He was talking faster than she could think. "Wow. You've thought of everything."

"I've always wanted to own a bar," Tex said. "A clean respectable little place. No BS and no tolerance for troublemakers. I'd like something to do in my years to come."

Ronny chewed on her Thumb nail. "When do you see this happening?"

"We need to get it all on paper. Run the numbers as they say. Clay's ready to go any time. He's been looking for a buyer a long time, but I never had someone I felt I could trust to go partners with me."

"Partners? You see me as a partner? Wow, I don't know what to say."

"It'll be fun until it's not. I know you'll make a

hand. I've seen that already. Did I tell you the name of the bar?"

"Hit me with it."

"Buds and Suds, get it?"

She chuckled. "I got it."

The location of the tile job loomed before them. The conversation ended, but Ronny knew it would continue.

Cassie hummed a tune as she made lunchmeat and cheese sandwiches. After her classes ended, she had straightened and cleaned the house. Ronny would be home from Harlingen around six-thirty. Tex kept a rigid schedule.

Sure enough, she burst through the door at six thirty.

"Honey, I'm home," she said, laughing.

Since they had come to Texas, Cassie had never seen her in such a good mood or so highly energized, sort of like one of those hurricanes blew in. "You must have had a good day. Installing tile must suit you."

"I've had an unbelievable day. Sister, you won't believe what I'm going to tell you."

"I've made sandwiches. Let's sit down and eat and you can tell me."

After Ronny told her everything, Cassie said. "That's wonderful and amazing and fantastic and I don't know any other words for it."

"I know. I still have to pinch myself to make sure I'm not dreaming."

"I'm sure I don't have to tell you if you do this, you'll have to stop calling this town *Lost* Tropicos. And you won't be able to go back to Tonawilla."

"And I sort of hate that. I always thought I might give Tommy Argyle another go. He makes good money and he's a good-looking sucker. Before we left, he was coming into the bar to visit me, saying he had some regrets about the divorce."

"You didn't tell me that. Did he say he had regrets about what he did that caused the divorce?"

Ronny shrugged. "What can I say? He's still interested."

"But you're not his only interest and that's a problem. Forget about him. He cheated on you and he would do it again."

Ronny shook her head. "I'm just talking. No, I'm sticking with Tex. He's a good friend. And he gets things done."

"You two are a good match. Whatever you do, I'm sure it will be great. When are you supposed to start work in the store?"

"Friday."

Cassie lifted her glass of tea in a toast. "To Friday."

CHAPTER 18

WHILE THE FOLLOWING week dragged for Cassie, for Ronny, time spun by faster than a whirlwind. Tex was ready to make a written offer on Clay and Elena's property. On Tuesday, he showed up with their financial records. Ronny and he both were pleasantly surprised to see the sizeable profit the little café/store/laundry/gas station made year after year.

"I knew this place was a money-maker," Tex said, his excitement moving the air around him. "I've been watching it for years. A little labor intensive, but no more than construction."

"Work doesn't scare me," Ronny replied. "I've always worked hard."

"Clay and Elena have waited a long time for a buyer. I've been holding my breath hoping some yahoo didn't come by and buy them out before I could pull a deal together. Clay wants cash and that much cash ain't easy to come by. I tried to tell him we should do some creative financing. As it is, his tax obligation will be a chunk. The government will get half his money."

"He told me he wanted cash," Ronny said. "That's

why I asked you to help me in the first place. I figured you could get a loan when I couldn't. Are you saying you aren't getting a loan? You're paying him cash?"

"I don't trust banks, darlin' and I don't like people prying into my personal life. Answering the questions on a loan application is just not in my comfort zone. I do it on construction projects because I have to, but I don't love it."

For Ronny, a new side of Tex emerged. She didn't know what nefarious life he might have once led to accumulate cash, but she was willing to let that lie in the past. She had worked with him and for him day after day, seen that he was a good man, never harmed anyone and worked hard sunup to sundown. So far, he had shown himself to be loyal. That was good enough for her.

"You've obviously got a buck or two. If you don't like banks, where do you put your money? A hole in the ground?"

He winked. "It's a secret, darlin'."

"Even if you don't like banks, we have to have a checking account. We'll have bills to pay. I don't relish taking a shovel to dig up the money in the yard."

"We only need one tiny business account."

"Okay. That will be enough."

She signed the partnership agreement drawn up by Paxton Atwater and just like that, she and Tex were business partners.

Excitement grew. With the ideas she had to improve store traffic and with the bar soon to be open next door, she would finally be an asset to some thing and not just a person hanging on from paycheck to paycheck. Life in Texas was proving to be lucky.

"Now that we've got a deal, you're going to have to start working alongside Elena," Tex said. "You gotta learn that business. When are you starting work in the café?"

"Friday."

"We won't get the deal finalized by then but go ahead and start learning everything you can about the nuts and bolts of that little operation."

In the short term, all she had to do was learn to cook. She could already run a retail store with her eyes closed.

Ever since Clay first approached her, Ronny had made a secret plan and kept it in the back of her mind. Now was the time for its trial run. "You know I don't know how to cook, don't you?"

"That's what you said. But I trust you'll learn."

"My little sister's a great cook."

"The schoolteacher?"

"Yep. Most of the decent meals I've ever eaten in my whole life came from her kitchen. She learned to cook trying to feed her asshole picky boyfriend. Once school is out in Tonawilla, New York, she won't have a job. I hope to persuade her to take over the kitchen and I'll do the store, like Clay and his wife do. Or did."

"It don't matter who cooks, darlin'. All that matters is that the food's good."

Meanwhile, Cassie was tied up every day with teaching. For the rest of the week, Ronny did the needed housework. She did every housekeeping chore she could think of from cleaning the bathroom to mopping the tile floors in the whole house. In her spare time, she did her nails.

Her first day in "Elena's Kitchen" turned out to be more than expected. She arrived at eight o'clock and found Elena and three helpers already busy. "Oops. Looks like I'm the ten o'clock scholar."

"No problem today," Elena said, "but you might want to think about coming in earlier."

Elena introduced her three helpers as Amelia Gonzalez, Sandra Gomez and Tania Villavazo. Two of them were chopping things and one was making *tortillas*.

"We serve everything fresh and from scratch," Elena explained. "Amelia and Sandra make the *salsa cruda* and the *salsa*. Tania makes the *tortillas.*"

While she was talking, Elena herself was cooking something on top of the stove in a huge cast iron skillet.

"What are you cooking?" Ronny asked.

"*Frijoles refritos.* Refried beans. I boiled the pinto beans yesterday and today I make the *frijoles refrito.*" She pointed to another large boiling pot on a back burner. "That's beans cooking for tomorrow's *refritos*. I cook them with bacon, onions, garlic, a little chili powder and salt. They have lots of flavor.

"Refried beans are a staple. They go with every serving of enchiladas or quesadillas and they go inside our *grande burritos*. Everyone who works with me in the kitchen learns how to make *frijoles refritos*. Come stand beside me. I show you. It's a simple dish."

As Ronny watched, Elena said, "We serve *Desayuno* and *Almuerzo*. Small, but filling meals."

"Sorry, but I don't speak Spanish," Ronny replied.

"That's okay," Elena said in perfect English. "That means breakfast and lunch. I use the Spanish words because that's what's written on our menu. We started out with that and we've never changed it. You can change it if you want to. Most of the customers are Anglos, but also, most of them speak a little bit of Spanish. They have to if they want to communicate. Probably ninety per cent of the population here is Hispanic."

"Ah, I see," Ronny said. "I'm sure I'll pick up on it. I'm a fast learner."

"First thing I do when I come in," Elena went on as she continued to stir the beans., "is get the morning's sweet rolls or muffins or whatever going. This morning, I made cinnamon rolls. I'm only able to make a few dozen. The same with muffins. They're almost all gone. We always sell out quickly."

The first question that passed through Ronny's mind was, *Are cinnamon rolls and muffins profitable enough to fool with?*

"I know what you're thinking," Elena said. "You're wondering if the sweet rolls and muffins are worth it. We pack them in boxes of four and six or someone can buy just one. Quick to grab on the way to work or whatever. We sell a box of six for twenty-two dollars and boxes of four for twenty dollars. They bring in a thousand dollars in revenue every day. I make them myself, so I'm not paying for labor."

"Do you ever make more?"

"No. We could sell more, but we don't have the

facilities or the room. Once you take over," Elena
went on, as she also continued to stir, "you might
want to consider a bigger stove and improving the
storage room.

"On the other hand, the cinnamon rolls and other
pastries are like the tamales. They're popular because
of the scarcity of them. Our old customers know
there are only so many, so they rush in to get them.

"They're important because they bring a customer
into the café who doesn't usually come in for our
Mexican food. Sometimes, while they're here for
blueberry muffins, they will pick up a few burritos
for breakfast. We make traditional breakfast burritos
the Anglo way. Scrambled eggs with sausage or ham."

Elena turned off the heat under the beans. "There.
Ready to serve."

And the day began.....

At lunchtime, Tex showed up to eat. After the rush
hour, Elena was able to break away from the kitchen
and she and Clay sat down with Ronny and Tex at a
corner table outside the traffic pattern.

Clay was anxious to get his retirement underway.
He had already chosen a motor home. He moved
through the operation's ins and outs faster than
Ronny could keep up, but Tex had no trouble.

CHAPTER 19

BY THE END of the day Ronny was as tired as she had ever been in her life. She left the café at eight o'clock with a handwritten cookbook in a spiral notebook. When she and Tex bought the café and store, Elena's secret recipes came with it. Elena had suggested she read and learn every recipe by memory.

At the little orange adobe house, she fell flat on her back onto the sofa, her long legs hanging over one arm. "I don't know if I'm capable of doing this," she told her sister.

"You've said that about everything you've ever tried. I think this is where someone says, you bought it, you own it."

"I was so excited I didn't think about how much work it would be. There's so much to learn. What if I've made a huge mistake? What if I fall on my ass?"

"Remember when you swore you'd never learn to drive a stick shift? You were going to quit driving altogether."

"That wasn't the same as this."

"How about skiing? You said if God had intended

people to ski, he would have made us with bigger feet."

Ronny shook her head. "Not the same."

"You called the Excel program, the devils diary, but you learned to use it. When you started bartending, you finally learned it only after trying to talk all the customers into having a beer failed."

"And the bartending gig would have been easier if it hadn't been for ladies' night'," Ronny groused. "If I never see a drink with an umbrella stuck in it again, it would be fine with me. But those fancy drinks don't matter. In Buds and Suds, we're going to serve beer and wine only. We won't even have a license to do anything else."

"The point I'm trying to make is every challenge in life you've met head on and I don't see you stopping now."

Ronny rose to her full stature. "You know what? You're right. I am friggin' amazing. I am woman. Hear me roar. There is nothing I can't do. Guess fatigue made me a little crazy for a minute."

Cassie laughed. "I'm glad we cleared that up. Next question. Are you going to get a gun?"

"What do you mean?"

"Mr. Thompson wears a gun. He says it keeps him from getting robbed. He says there's no law enforcement locally."

Ronny's heart made a little skip. She knew all of that. A visual of her strolling around the café wearing a gun like Clay was comical. "I don't know. You know I can't shoot. I doubt if it's legal to have a gun in the bar. I'll have to discuss it with Tex. He has guns, but he doesn't wear one. Can you see me with a gun?"

"No, but you probably should think about it."

"Hah. Bad-ass Ronny with a gun on her hip. That's me."

"Actually, that *is* you. That brings me to another question. Does Tex know you can't cook?"

"More or less. I told him I wasn't a domestic goddess."

"That isn't the same as saying 'I can't cook'"

"Okay, okay, I told him I can't cook. He said the only thing that's important is that the food is good." Ronny dropped back to the sofa and dragged the recipe book off the floor, fanned the pages. "Just look at all of these recipes I have to learn. I have to cram everything into my head before Elena and Clay leave."

Cassie took the book and thumbed through it. "Some of these dishes look sooo good."

"Elena doesn't serve food like most restaurants. Her menu is limited. For breakfast, she makes three different kinds of burritos. Piles of them. Mostly, people buy them to take with them."

"Take out?"

"Yep. The first thing I thought of was there should be a drive-up window. Maybe Tex could fix that. Elena also makes sweet rolls of some kind every day. She goes in at four o'clock in the morning and makes them. Today, she made cinnamon rolls and oh, my God, they were so good. Clay says they're better than Cinnabon's. They were almost all gone by the time I got there at eight o'clock this morning."

Cassie sighed. "When was the last time we had a Cinnabon's cinnamon roll?"

"The last time we went to see our cousin in the

city." Ronny shot her a serious look from beneath
her brow. "Missing New York yet?"

"Don't get excited. New York City isn't the only
place that has Cinnabon's. Are you going to learn to
make cinnamon rolls and go in at four o'clock?"

"I'll have to. I want to do everything exactly like
Elena does."

"You've obviously got your work cut out for you,
Sister."

"I know. That's what has me scared."

"What does she sell for lunch?"

"The employees make the lunches. Cheese, chicken
or beef enchiladas. Tacos—might be any kind. We
aren't that far from the ocean. She can get fresh-
caught shrimp or crab—anything like that—straight
from the Gulf of Mexico. And if she does, she makes
shrimp tacos. People seem to love shrimp tacos. And
a couple of different kinds of nachos.

"She puts one of those sandwich board signs
outside with the day's menu on it. When I got there
this morning, customers were lined up. Elena says
there are a few customers who eat there every single
day."

"Wow, that is different all right. I can't believe we've
never eaten there."

"Let's face it. It's captive customers. The only game
in town and no one likes to cook at home anymore.
Tomorrow, Clay's going to teach me how to repair
the washers and dryers." She thrust her hands forward,
her fingers splayed. "Do these look like the hands of
an appliance repair person? My nails! Think about
my nails!"

"Oh, the horror," Cassie said. "Cooking and

cleaning in the kitchen every day, think about that acrylic on your fingertips."

Ronny clasped both sides of her head with her hands and shook her head. "And after the laundry repair lessons, Elena's going to teach me how to make sauces out of dried peppers."

Grinning, Cassie pushed back from the table and the computer that had held her attention until Ronny came in. "All of this is going to take some energy, but I have faith in you."

"I should probably start going to mass."

Cassie laughed. "You're a trip, Sister. Mass is always a good idea." She heaved a great breath. "Okay then. While I grab a quick shower would you start dinner?"

"Are you kidding me? I've been cooking all day. I'll grab the shower and *you* cook. At least you know how."

As Ronny allowed the hot cascade of water to ease the tight muscles in her shoulders, for the first time, the weight of the responsibility she had undertaken impacted her and she began to tremble.

Dear God, if you'll just let things work out, I promise I'll start going to mass.

The unmistaken aroma of grilling meat teased her nostrils and made her stomach twist in hunger. Though she had been surrounded by good food all day, she hadn't thought about eating.

When she reappeared in the kitchen, their small table was set with plates and eating utensils and neatly folded sheets of paper towel as napkins. A hamburger patty and a bun lay on each plate. Another plate of lettuce leaves, slice tomatoes and sliced onions sat in the middle of the table. Also jars of pickles, mayonnaise and a squeeze bottle of mustard.

"Ready to eat Miss Up-and-Coming Entrepreneur?" Cassie asked, a big smile on her face.

Ronny spread her hands, showing her palms. "Wow. Looks delicious. Looks like a chef got loose in our kitchen."

A dubious look came from Cassie. "Stop it, Ronny. It's hamburgers."

Ronny ignored her sarcasm. "And iced tea, huh? Hanging out with Bo, you've made a total conversion."

"Shut up, Ronny, and sit down while the hamburger patties are still warm. You know that sweet tea is what they drink down here."

Ronny sat and reached for the mustard. "You've become quite the little homemaker again. Real plates, silverware, home cooking. Pampering Bo like you used to pamper Frank. Being in love suits you."

Cassie took a seat and reached for the mayonnaise. "It's different with Bo. He pampers me back. And I never said I was in love."

As they each built a burger, Ronny talked. "Maybe not, but when you talk about him, you use words like 'wonderful' and 'no one in the world is like him.' All the years you spent with that ass-hat Frank, you never had the glow you have now. Even back home, after that weekend you and he were snowed in together at that Vince Lombardi Service Area."

"In Frank's defense," Cassie said, "we weren't alone. There was also a truck driver, a teenage couple and a hitchhiker. He terrified all of us. Not exactly a romantic rendezvous."

"Okay, that wasn't the best example, but you've

never had such an *air* about you. You look happy, dare I say content?"

Ronny picked up her burger and bit into it. Juices dripped onto the plate. Ronny grabbed a sheet of paper towel and quickly wiped her mouth. "Oh, wow, Cass. This is delicious. Better than McDonald's."

"We are not going to talk about content. Let's say happy and leave it at that." Cassie tossed a dishtowel at her sister's head.

Laughing, Ronny caught it. "We *are* happy aren't we? And if we're not, we should be. I've got a life-changing opportunity and you're in love with a terrific guy and he's crazy about you." She took another bite of her hamburger. "Oh, man, Cassie, you've really outdone yourself. This is a delicious hamburger."

Cassie swallowed and made a little gasp. "You made it yourself. So why with the flowery BS about the food. Spill it. What're you really getting at?"

"Well....I've been thinking."

Cassie sat back in her chair and crossed her arms over her chest. "Every time you say that, I get nervous."

Ronny cocked her head and opened her palms. "Look, didn't I listen to your idea about trying to raise cows with steers? And I came to Texas with you, didn't I?"

"Kicking and screaming the whole way."

"I've got an idea."

Cassie's attention returned to her own burger. "I knew it," she said around a mouthful of food. "You're going to try to talk me into something, aren't you? Okay, I'm listening."

She always listened. That was one of the many things Ronny loved about her little sister. "When school's out, you come and work in the café."

Cassie wiped her mouth. "Wait tables? No, absolutely not. I fully intend to get my Texas teaching certificate. Bo says they're so desperately short of teachers they're even bringing in people with no degree."

Ronny shook her head. "No, no. Not wait tables. You can cook. I'll work the bar and mind the store. And help in the kitchen, too, of course."

A severe frown creased Cassie's brow. "Are you crazy, Ronny? I know nothing about cooking in a café and I know even less about cooking Mexican food."

"Look, Elena and Clay won't be hitting the road for another two or three weeks. They've agreed to stay on and help me in the store and the café until they leave. We could both learn a lot from them in three weeks."

"Mmph," Cassie mumbled, chewing.

Time for a different tactic. "Okay, then. Think about this. If you intend to teach, you're going to have to do it in Harlingen and that's forty-five miles away, one way.

"I know that. I'm trying to figure it out."

"You can't drive that damn taco truck. We'd have to get another car. A reliable one. An expense we can't afford."

Cassie drew a deep breath. "I know that, too."

"I'm not saying you shouldn't get that teaching certificate if that's what you want to do. I'm just asking you to help me out a little bit. I mean, I'm your sister."

Cassie stopped eating and shot her one of her doubtful looks.

"Think about it, Cass. This is a good opportunity for both of us. And you can understand Spanish."

"And understanding a little Spanish makes me able to cook Mexican food? That makes no sense."

"You're smart. You can learn."

Cassie drummed her fingers on the table. "Those recipes do look good. It would be a challenge."

"What's life without a challenge?"

"I'll think about it."

Ronny did a mental fist pump. Life just got sweeter. If Cassie said she would think about it, she would probably do it. A wave of sentimentality passed through Ronny. Life had always been a struggle for her and Cassie, but they had always stuck together. They had lost their mom much too soon and now, life, full of surprises, had deposited them in the end of the world, but they were still together.

"You know what?"

"What?" Cassie asked.

"I haven't thanked Tex. He's made this possible and I think I was in too much shock to really express my gratitude. I'm calling him now." Leaving the table, she reached across the couch and grabbed her cell phone.

"So there *is* something between you two? You seem to get along great but you haven't really said anything about how you feel. Are there sparks?"

"Nah." Ronny returned to the table, pressed in numbers. She spoke as the phone burred. "He's like my brother. It is so refreshing to not be hit on."

She stopped when Tex came on the line. "Tex Barton. Speak yer piece, Yankee."

"Hi, Tex. It just occurred to me that I haven't thanked you for what you are doing for me. I never had a father and when a male does something good for me it always meant something other than kindness. You've given me a chance to actually have a life instead of just going day to day trying to live one. I had no direction and not much hope. You are a special person. I haven't known you long, but I want you to know there's nothing I wouldn't do for you. You're like the brother I've never had."

Silence on the other end of the line.

"Hello?...Hello?...Tex, are we still connected?"

"Who is this?" Tex finally said.

"Who is this? Who *is* this? I can count on one hand the times I've poured my heart out in gratitude and all you can say is 'who is this'? You're an ass. If you were on fire, I'd throw gasoline on you. The only thing bigger than your precious Texas is your ego!"

"Now darlin' you can cuss me all you want to, but I can't listen to you talk bad about my Texas. You gonna be at the store tomorrow?"

"Of course."

"Then I'll catch you there. We've got some things to go over. See you later, alligator." He disconnected.

Ronny clapped the phone down on the table and looked straight into Cassie's eyes. "God help any woman who might fall in love with him. He makes me want to pull out all my eyelashes."

CHAPTER 20

CASSIE FLOATED ON a cloud the rest of the week. Bo would be home Saturday night. He had called and told her to plan to go to supper and a movie in Harlingen on Sunday. She was still amused by the way he called the evening meal "supper" instead of "dinner." Every time she heard it, she had to stop and think about the time of day they would be eating.

At the same time those thoughts had taken root, she couldn't get the idea of working in the Mexican food kitchen out of her head and the fact that Ronny needed her. That was opposite from the way things were usually. Usually, Cassie needed Ronny.

Due to a teachers' meeting in Tonawilla, classes on Thursday were canceled. Cassie decided to go to the café with Ronny, even if it did mean she had to fall out of bed at 3:00 a.m. so Ronny could be there at 4:00 a.m.

"I heard you coming," Elena said, laughing when they entered the cafe. She was just getting started with cheese blintzes, which would be sold today as well as doughnuts. "We'll sell a lot of these today, so we'll make a lot."

"You remember cheese blintzes, don't you?" Ronny asked Cassie. "We used to get them when we went into the city."

Cheese blintzes was a classic Jewish pastry. Anyone even close to New York City knew of them. "Of course, I do," Cassie replied.

"Would you believe I now know how to make them?"

With pride, Cassie smiled up at her big sister. "I'm proud of you, Sister."

Elena had already started assigning different tasks to her three helpers. Besides prepping and cooking the pastries, lunchtime prep had to be done also.

After she finished, she turned to Cassie. "When we make blintzes, we make six dozen. We cook the crepes and the filling a day ahead so that on the day we sell them, all we have to do is fry them and they're fresh."

She pointed toward one of her helpers who was busy crushing raspberries in a large saucepan. "We also offer a little cup of raspberry sauce with each blintz. I ask my girls to strain the seeds out of it. A lot of customers have false teeth. They don't like or can't eat the seeds."

"Amelia is the doughnut maker," Ronny told Cassie. "I've helped her once. I'm going to help her again. Want to watch?"

"My goodness, Ronny," Cassie said, watching Ronny carefully measure ingredients into a huge electric mixer's bowl. "This is quite an operation.

Who would have ever thought a little café in the middle of nowhere would sell so much food?"

"People come from all parts of Cameron County and beyond," Elena said. "It has taken years for Clay and me to build this clientele.

"I know blintzes aren't native to South Texas," she went on, "but once people eat them, they like them. What's not to like? Sweetened cream cheese inside a crisp crust. I started out experimenting with a couple dozen and the demand took off. They go hand in hand with our other delicious breakfast items."

"Which are?" Cassie asked. "Something besides muffins and cinnamon rolls?"

"Some days we offer an assortment of Mexican pastries. I make them from *mi madre's* recipe. *Peine*, for example. It's made of puff pastry filled with jam or jelly, sort of like American bear claws. *Empanadas*, with either fruit in season, or pumpkin. *Empanadas* in Mexican food go back to the sixteenth century.

"*Picón*, which is a cone-shaped bread with three points on one of its ends, covered with an egg, sugar and lard-based custard; *Pollo*, Brioche-style bread filled with custard or confectioner's cream and sprinkled with powdered sugar.

"And our Mexican pastry offering wouldn't be complete without *conchas*, the most common pastry in all of Mexico. Everyone loves."

"Wow, that's a lot of stuff," Cassie said.

"Oh, we don't offer all of those things at once, but whatever we make, we always sell out. We could sell more, but just like with the doughnuts and cinnamon rolls, we've only got so much space."

"Just think how much more traffic we're going to

generate after Tex puts in his little sports bar," Ronny said.

Cassie recognized an arm twist when she felt one. Ronny was good at that.

"You should probably add at least one more person in the kitchen," Elena advised. "You'll want to make things people can nibble on while they watch the games. Things that go with beer. Maybe good seasoned popcorn and nuts or tasty homemade dips and chips. *Nachos* all day long. My recipe for *nachos* is the best. You'll need an extra person to make all those things."

Cassie had an almost uncontrollable yen to jump into the middle of the cooking. Minute by minute, working to help Ronny was taking on more appeal.

"Elena thinks we should change the name of the café," Ronny said. "Not right away, of course. She thinks if we worked as partners, we could call it '*Dos Hermanas*'. Or just '*Hermanas*.'"

"'Two Sisters?'"

"Just a thought," Elena replied. "You probably wouldn't want to call it 'Elena's Kitchen.'"

Careful not to commit herself, Cassie shook her head. "I don't know. It's been 'Elena's Kitchen' for a long time. Seems like a good marketing idea to leave it as it is."

The day progressed. As the lunch menu prep continued, Cassie was ready to dive in with both hands and feet. They prepared beef and cheese enchiladas and chicken enchiladas with green sauce, all made from scratch. As a second option, they offered *quesadillas* made with *frijoles refritos* and three different kinds of cheese.

Cassie could see that the little café was a huge amount of work if Ronny and Tex intended for it to continue as Clay and Elena Thompson had run it. How could it be successful otherwise?

Ronny, who had never really learned to cook anything very complicated, needed help badly. Who better to help her than her little sister? In their whole lives, Ronny had never called on Cassie for much. In spite of herself, Cassie began to re-think her plan to work as an educator.

The next morning, standing at the kitchen sink sipping her coffee, Cassie looked out the window over the sink. She had been up since 4:00 a.m, after the mariachi music from the taco truck awakened her at 3:30. Ronny going to work at the café. She hadn't been able to go back to sleep, so she just got up. They really needed to do something about that music from the taco truck.

Outside, the brilliant sun was rising on a glorious balmy morning. A bougainvillea climbed up the courtyard wall, displaying its copious and beautiful blood-red blooms against the orange wall, a colorful sight. She had never seen a bougainvillea plant until she came here, had never seen a palm tree, had never eaten shrimp fresh-caught from the Gulf of Mexico.

As she did every day, she checked the weather app on her cell phone for New York weather. One of the last ties she hadn't broken. A squall, even snow, was

forecast. She couldn't keep from chuckling. *Really,
New York?*

If she were back in Tonawilla, instead of shorts, a
T-shirt and flip-flops, she would be wearing a heavy
sweater and knee-high boots. There would still be
skiing in the mountains. Not that she cared about
that. She had never learned to ski.

She switched to weather in Harlingen, Texas. Today,
the temperature would be around eighty.

Not even once, despite the inconveniences she and
Ronny had learned to live with, had she regretted
coming to Texas. Indeed, the last three months had
brought many firsts into her and Ronny's lives. And
she had met a guy who, other than gender, resembled
Frank on no way.

Sighing, she poured herself another cup of coffee,
her third. She added another spoonful of creamer and
sipped. Sometimes she thought she might be more
addicted to the creamer than the coffee. Currently
she was hooked on sweet Italian cream, the only one
she had found in Thompson's grocery store.

She mulled over helping Ronny in the café. She
was so pleased that Ronny had this opportunity,
Cassie couldn't refuse to help her. She actually liked
working in the little café's kitchen, had loved learning
to make cheese blintzes, followed by learning to make
enchiladas.

She had more or less committed to help her sister.

Though a part of her feared giving up teaching and
a steady paycheck, the thought of a new endeavor
held a powerful appeal. In the past three months, she
had become braver than she ever thought she could
be.

They had even discussed how she could become a full partner if she decided to stick with it. Now, myriad questions tumbled through her mind, among them, what if the café didn't make enough money to afford to replace her teacher's salary?

What if it didn't even make enough month to pay Tex back?

What if Clay and Elena Thompson's steady stream of customers didn't transfer their loyalty to Ronny? On the other hand, how could they not? Like Ronny said, Elena's Kitchen was the only restaurant for miles.

She wouldn't make a final decision until she discussed the cafe with Bo tomorrow.

Turning from the sink she took a seat at the kitchen table and organized her material for another day of teaching. The long-distance teaching was working wonderfully for both her and her students.

She contemplated each day as if the ban on school attendance would be lifted, but unlike Texas, the state of New York still maintained high COVID numbers. She felt sure the quarantine would last to the end of the current school year.

She opened her laptop and logged in. A message blazed across the screen. *Due to a power outage, there will be no school today.*

Cripes. Now what?

She glanced up at the two sconces that flanked the fireplace and provided light in the living room/kitchen area. A bulb burned in only one. She left her chair and found a new bulb in one of the kitchen drawers, walked over to the sconce, rose up on her tiptoes and screwed the old bulb out of the socket.

With an ever so slight hum, the back wall of the

fireplace smoothly glided open, revealing a dark maw.

Her breath caught. Her eyes bugged. For a full minute, she stared in shock and astonishment. "Oh, my gosh," she finally whispered.

Fearfully, as if she expected something supernatural to appear, she looked around, then stared into the dark opening again.

Squinting, she could see vague shapes but couldn't make out what they were. She could feel cool air. *Air conditioning?*

She strode to a drawer in the kitchen cabinet and picked out a flashlight, returned to the opening, shined the light inside. "Hello?" she called into the darkness. "Hello?...Hello?...."

The opening was more than large enough to walk through. First, she leaned forward and peered into it. Saw nothing she could make out. With great care, she stepped through the opening, found herself on a concrete landing with descending stairs going forward. Shining the flashlight onto the walls, to her left, she saw a group of switches. She flipped one and the door began to glide closed.

"No! No, don't!" she cried, quickly turning back to the door.

She thrust her arm through the shrinking opening, trying to stop the door, but it was too powerful. It was about to crush her arm. She yanked her arm back just in time. The door silently closed tightly, leaving her with nothing but a weak flashlight beam in the blackest darkness and the most profound silence she had ever known.

Don't panic, don't panic. She flipped the wall switch again. Up and down. Up and down.

Nothing.

She rapidly flipped the switches again. "Please. Come on…"

Envisioning how thoroughly the fireplace wall hid the opening to this abyss and the fact that no one knew it existed, tears rushed to her eyes. No one would find her and rescue her. She would suffocate. She would die.

"No! Please, God…"

Frantically, she banged on the door with her fist. "Help!...Help!...Please!..."

She stopped. Who would hear her? Ronny would be at the café most of the day. Even if she were home, could she hear cries for help?

Then it dawned on her that she felt cool air. Cool, breathable air. She wouldn't suffocate after all.

"Okay, calm down," Cassie mumbled to herself. She would simply call Ronny and tell her of her dilemma.

She reached for her pocket. And froze. Her heartbeat took off like a shot. When she left her chair to change the lightbulb, she had left the phone on the table beside her computer.

OhmyGod. No, no, no, no…. Mother of God, damnit to hell and sonuvabitch.

"Don't cuss, Cassie" she mumbled. "And don't panic. You'll give yourself a heart attack. You're okay. You've got light and air."

She sank to sit on the landing to try to think through her situation. Was she in a cave? A tunnel? If it was a tunnel, where did it go? It had to have an end.

The flashlight's glow began to dim. To save the light

for when she might need it more, she switched it off quickly, leaving herself in stygian darkness.

Tears burned again, but she swallowed them back, not wanting to cry. She gave a nervous titter. Ronny had always called her a crybaby, said she cried about everything.

Stop being such a crybaby. You've got to get tougher."

"*I'm tough," Cassie had argued.*

"*No, you're not. You're a cream puff."*

She sniffed away tears. She loved her sister so much. What would they have done over the years without each other? Tears burned her eyes again. Would she ever see Ronny again?

Her memory spun even further back to the two days back in New York when she had been stranded in a blizzard until a state cop rescued her. She had been so terrified.

But not as terrified as she was now.

At one point she dozed. She awoke with a start. Had she heard a noise? Or had she dreamed it? She fumbled for the flashlight and switched it back on.

She looked around again. Mounted on the wall beside the bank of switches was a plastic shield she hadn't seen before. She could tell it provided protection for a note, written in bold letters and posted above a small box of numbers: *FOR ENTRY PRESS IN THE CODE AND HOLD THE LAST NUMBER FOR THREE SECONDS*

Code?

Code! Oh, thank God, there's a code!

But what is it?

The day she and Ronny were given a tour of their new surroundings, the attorney had told them many things but nothing about a dark cave with a code. Did he know about this place and if he did, why hadn't he said something? All he had said was the fireplace hadn't been used in years and probably didn't work.

She checked her watch. Noon. Ronny was usually home by four o'clock. But so what? If she banged on the door again with her fist, would Ronny hear her?

Tears rushed to her eyes again, but she swiped them away with the back of her hand.

She was hungry. Breakfast had been a piece of toast and three cups of coffee. Even if she didn't die from suffocation, she would starve.

In front of her, the stairs went on without an obvious end. No point in going backward. She summoned her courage and gingerly, with hope in her heart, stepped off the landing, onto the first step.

Along the wall on the left side lightbulbs were strung, but how could she get them to turn on? She had already flipped every switch she could find.

Following the string of light bulbs, she eventually came to a switch box. It was in the *Off* position. On a prayer, she flipped it to *On*. A sudden burst of light nearly blinded her for a few seconds. A great breath of relief rushed from her chest and she switched off the flashlight. The light from it was waning anyway.

She looked around, awestruck. She was definitely in a tunnel and in full light. It was more than four feet wide and would easily accommodate the tallest of anyone she knew. Wood paneling lined the walls and ceiling. It appeared to be well built. With air and electricity and concrete stair steps, someone had spent a lot of money constructing this.

A dawning came to her. They were close to Mexico.

This was a smuggler's path from Mexico into the U.S. And it was how the two women Ronny found in the living room got into their house. Who knew what else came through this passageway? The people who traversed it obviously knew the code for opening the fireplace wall.

Oh, dear God. People smuggling. Drug cartels. Guns. Drugs and guns. Her heartbeat quickened again.

For a second, she thought about turning back. But maybe not. She had now walked quite a distance from the fireplace and from what she could tell there was more tunnel ahead. Maybe the tunnel went to another house, to a barn. Or to a door through which she could escape.

She continued walking, aware she was going deeper into the earth. She stopped every few steps and listened for noise of any kind. She heard nothing but her own labored breathing. How long had she been walking?

Suddenly, ahead she thought she saw the wished-for door. Nothing as fancy as the sliding door behind her. Just a plain wooden door. A guarded sense of relief washed through her.

CHAPTER 21

RONNY DROVE LIKE a bat out of hell to get home, the mariachi music blaring across the countryside. Elena had taught her the Spanish words to *El Rancho Grande* and she sang along with the trumpets and guitars, belting out the words with accompanying hand gestures. "*Ay ay ay ay…Mama no me dijo nada…Mama no me dijo nada… Solo me hablo de amor…Ay ay ay ay…*"

Elena hadn't taught her precisely what the words meant in English, but she had said it was a love song. Something about being alone and belting out a song to the wide-open spaces without worrying about who you might disturb was stress-relieving.

At the same time, she told herself, they had to do something about that damn music. Having people stop on the street and stare was embarrassing. The truck wasn't a bad vehicle and seemed to be reliable. She had learned to handle the stick shift all right and was even managing the lack of power steering.

She couldn't wait to tell Cassie that Tex had started construction on the bar. She had tried to call her several times through the day, but the calls had gone to voice mail. *Damn hit or miss Wi-Fi.*

Back in New York, they'd had reliable Internet. Here, even a thirty-foot pole with a dish on top had not made Wi-Fi a hundred percent reliable.

Not being able to reach her sister all day nagged at her and left her nerves on edge. Or as Cassie would say, at her bitchy best.

She herded the taco truck into the barn, got out and picked up the broom she kept beside the doorway. No way did she intend to cross the backyard without sweeping it and beating it for snakes. So far, she hadn't seen one, but that didn't mean they weren't there just waiting to bite her.

She entered the house through the back doorway into the kitchen, loudly complaining she'd had a hard day and most things hadn't gone as planned. The lights were on. Cassie's laptop and all of her teaching stuff were spread over their only table.

"Hey, Cass, guess what."

She walked through the house to the bedrooms and back. Silence. No Cassie. She strode through the front doorway and out into the courtyard.

"Hey, Cass. Come out, come out, wherever you are."

Still no Cassie.

She punched in Bo's number, hoping he was home. He answered on the first burr. "Hi, cowboy. This is Ronny Jennings. Is Cassie with you?"

"No. I just got home. I'm picking her up tomorrow. We're going to Harlingen for supper and a movie."

"Ha-ha. Is that the same as dinner and a movie?"

"Yup."

"The way you Texans talk kills me. Anyway, I can't find Cassie anywhere. If she's not with you, I don't know where she could be. I've had the taco truck in town all day, so she couldn't have gone anywhere on wheels."

"Did you look around outside?"

"That's where I am now."

"Sit tight. I'll come over."

Cassie hesitated. What would she say if someone answered her knock? *Hi, I just happened to be in the area. . . . Could I perhaps borrow a cup of sugar?*

Squaring her shoulders and heaving a great breath, she knocked on the door. *Rap-rap-rap!*

Before she finished the third rap, the door swung open. A Mexican man cradling a large gun confronted her. Her heart fell to her feet and her breath caught.

He grinned, one front tooth gleaming with gold. "What have we here? A *pequeño pedero cordita?* Come inside, *mi cordero pegueño.*"

Oh, please God! What in hell have I stumbled into and how am I going to get out?

Visualizing herself roasting on a spit, Cassie gulped. "I—I know what you said. It means little lost lamb. I'm not lost and I'm not your little lamb."

"Ahhh. *Hablas español.* This is good."

His grin turned to a menacing grimace as he gestured her inside with a head tilt.

The big gun he cradled like a baby told her she had no other option. He held the door open and even

though he hadn't pointed the gun at her directly, its
presence had the effect she was sure he expected.

She edged past him into a crudely furnished room.
Two young, bedraggled women huddled together on
a tattered blanket on the filthy floor. They stared at
her with sad, but vacant eyes. Were they drugged?

Her captor picked up a curl of her hair. "*Chica
blanca bonita.* You will bring me *mucho dinero.*"

Oh, my God. He intends to sell me!

Her first instinct was to run. How and where, she
didn't know. She jerked her head away.

The women hugged each other even more tightly
and began to murmur.

Women? They weren't women. They were female
all right, but in reality, they were no older than
teenagers, maybe even younger than that. Even
lifeless from drugs, they were terrified. She had never
witnessed this depth of human emotion and was
amazed how contagious it could be. She was terrified
herself.

Her jaw clenched. She would die before she allowed
herself to become like those girls. It took everything
she had to pull her shoulders back and look directly
into the eyes of the man holding a gun, his finger
on the trigger. Beyond her control, a nervous grin
twitched a corner of her mouth.

"You think this funny?" He let go of the gun long
enough to pat his chest with one hand. "You think I
am just some greaser playing *hombre grande*? I watch
this house for months. I no see the *gringo viejo* no
more, but he did good job making it look like a
burned-out house.

"No one even notice it but me. *I* notice it." He

patted his chest again. "My own boss don' know what I been doing, but when I tell him what I found, he will give me my own crew. He will give me new truck and new house filled with food for my family for years."

With squinted eyes, she studied him. He was younger than she was, not much taller than her fifth-grade students and unbelievably thin. His English was broken, but fair. Had he been educated in the U.S.? She saw fear in his eyes. Still, machismo dripped from his every pore.

Play the part, play the part, play the part, Cassie told herself. If she ever wanted to see Ronny or Bo again, she had to stay cool and be smart. Her insides were shaking, but she mustered a strong voice. "I wasn't laughing at you or the situation. My name's Cassie, but a lot of my friends call me Cass. I'm a teacher and you remind me of one of my students. His name is—"

"Shut up!" The gunman thrust his face within inches of hers.

Her shoulders scrunched and her teeth clamped tightly.

"*Te llamas* mean nothing to me," he shouted. "Or anything about you. I wan' to know how you get here."

She believed communication was the way to end conflict. She steeled herself and in her head, put together a sentence in Spanish. "*Por favor dime tu nombre.* I need to know your name. So we can talk."

"I am Agapito," he answered in a calmer voice.

"Aww. I know what that means. One who is

cherished. Your mother must have loved you very much."

"Shut up. We talk English. How you get here?"

"By accident. And I don't have the code to get out or I wouldn't be here."

"Code? What you mean code?"

"I suppose this tunnel starts somewhere in Mexico. At the other end, in Texas, there's a door that can only be opened by typing in a code. Someone in Mexico has to give the code to whoever comes in here."

She looked over at the two half-conscious women propped up against the wall. "It was probably given to them, but they're so out of it they don't know anything. I don't see how they could have walked in on their own. Did you carry them?"

The man spit on the floor and sneered. "They are nothing. They are *putas*, I will sell them."

Whores? Cassie wanted to cry, but she reinforced her will. "They're kids. Younger than you and me. Have you no shame?"

"*Putas*," he repeated. He walked over to one of the girls and kicked her foot, "Hey, wake up." Getting little response, he gave a forceful kick to her knee. The girl cried out and began to sniffle.

"Stop that!" Cassie cried. "It's your fault they're practically unconscious. What did you give them?"

"It was nothing. They scream and all that shit. They wake up in a few hours."

"A few hours? Did you say a few hours? I can't stay here for hours. You need to know something. There are people looking for me."

He glared at her with narrowed eyes. "Who? Who look for you?"

"My sister. She'll turn the earth flat looking for me. And my boyfriend."

"Aha. They find us both."

"You're lost?"

Agapito didn't answer her question. He reached in his pocket and retrieved a cell phone; tossed it to Cassie. "Call your sister. Tell her you fine and want to be home later. And don't do nothing cute."

Cassie looked at the phone. Dare she be excited? This was her sliver of a chance to somehow get the message to Ronny that she was in trouble. When she did nothing, Agaito finally asked, "What is wrong?"

Cassie answered dismally "I, uh, well,…I don't know her number from memory. I had it stored in the phone I left behind."

Agapito laughed, then walked over and yanked his phone out of her hand. "You go into a *túnel* with no phone? And now, you don' know phone numbers?" He pointed a finger at her nose. "You not very smart."

She batted his finger away. "You haven't been all the way through the tunnel? You came into it and you don't know where it goes? You're the one who isn't very smart."

"What this *túnel* for?"

"I don't know. Maybe it was built to transport someone or something illegal into Texas."

"How far is Texas?"

"I don't know. I know it's a long walk back. Very dark. Cool and kind of creepy. Kind of like being in a grave or—"

"Shut up!" he yelled.

She jumped. Clearly, she had struck a chord.

No one had ever yelled at her or threatened her.

Suddenly, from out of nowhere, as if some mystic cloak of confidence and power had settled upon her shoulders, she no longer feared him. "What did you give those girls? What if they die from what you gave them? Then what will you do?"

"They die. You die, too. I go back where I come from. You? No one will find you."

Ronny paced the courtyard. Her confidence level of her sister's well-being had fled like a flock of birds.

A vehicle stopped outside and Bo strode into the courtyard. "Did you find her?"

Ronny stood slack- jawed, her palms open. "Do you see her?"

Bo pulled his phone from his pocket. "I'll call her again."

From inside the house, the sultry voice of Cassie's latest music obsession, Patsy Cline, filled the air singing "Crazy," her ring choice for Bo's calls. Cassie had told Ronny earlier that particular song had meaning for her and Bo.

Now, it hauntingly vibrated off the walls of the little orange house.

"Oh, my God," Bo said, looking at her with widened eyes. "She doesn't have her phone."

"That's about the size of it," Ronny said, fighting back tears. "She wouldn't leave without her phone. *Fuck!* Where in the hell is she?...Sorry. I tend to cuss when I'm upset"

Ronny swallowed and wiped her eyes with the back of her hand. "Should we call the cops?"

Bo's head shook. "They won't do anything about a missing person until she's been missing forty-eight hours."

"But we're so close to the border and we're isolated here."

"Have you talked to Tex? Maybe he knows something we don't."

"That's not possible. I've been with him all day. But it *has* been an hour since I left him. Maybe he does know something."

Ronny pressed Tex's number into her phone. When he answered, she explained the concern she and Bo had.

"There's gotta be a good explanation," Tex said. "Let me finish up what I'm doing here and I'll head your way."

After they disconnected, Bo said, "I'm gonna make a call."

He pressed in some numbers and waited. Then, "Bo Buckalew here....I've got a missing person....Possibly a kidnap victim.....No, haven't involved the local authorities. This is personal.....Name is Cassandra Grace Jennings. Blond, blue-eyed, curly hair. Petite. Twenty-eight years old.... I understand....I want to see some action....Do what you can."

He disconnected. Ronny had listened to that conversation and watched him with suspicious eyes. "Wait a minute. Are you a cop?"

"Uh, I just know a few people in law enforcement."

"You said kidnap victim." The words rushed out of Ronny with a huff. More tears fought for release.

"Oh, my God, Bo. Do you think my sister could have been kidnapped? How often do women just disappear around here? I've heard the stories about kidnapped women being sold into slavery." Ronny couldn't hold back sobs. "It can't be true."

Bo reached out and brought her close, patted her shoulder while she cried against his chest. "Let's don't jump to conclusions. We—"

Ra-tat-tat! Ra-tat-tat! Ra-tat-tat!...

A deafening sound like staccato gunfire erupted from the fireplace. The back wall of the fireplace ripped open and crashed to the floor in pieces. The smell of cordite and dust filled the air.

Ronny's jaw dropped. Her tears dried.

"Jesus!" Bo said.

A Mexican man with a big gun shoved Cassie through the jagged opening. She had one arm around a ragged young woman's waist, practically dragging her across the debris. A second woman hung onto her.

"Cassie!" Ronny and Bo cried in unison and stepped forward.

"Do not move!" The gun-wielding man pointed his weapon at Cassie. "I shoot her."

CHAPTER 22

R ONNY AND BO stopped in their tracks.
    "Ronny, stay calm," Bo said in a level voice.
    "Calm?" Ronny shouted. "Cassie, are you all right?
Who are these girls? How did you run into a bandit?"
    "Shut the fuck up!" the bandit shouted.
    "If you do anything to my sister, I swear—"
    "Ronny, please," Cassie pleaded, "don't make
matters worse."
    "How the fuck can I make matters worse?" Ronny
yelled, throwing up a hand. "You've just stepped in
from a giant hole in our wall with two strange girls
and a bandit with a gun and you want me to stay
calm?"
    "Ronny, cool it," Bo said firmly from behind her.
    The bandit took a tighter grip on Cassie's arm and
pushed her closer, pointed his gun directly at Ronny.
"I will not tell you shut up one more time. Better I
kill you than hear you."
    He dropped his hold on Cassie's arm, took a step
back and raised his gun to shoulder level, pointed at
Ronny.

Oh, my God. I'm going to die. God, I'm sorry I didn't go to mass more often.

The small living room suddenly seemed smaller. The smell of body odors mixed with adrenaline and fear permeated the room. Ronny's head swam, she longed to sit down and close her eyes to it all. She clamped her mouth shut and backed up.

The bandit's focus shifted to Bo. "You, Ranger. Your gun. And the one in your boot, too. I know all your tricks. I know more about you, Ranger, than you know about me."

"Ranger? How did baseball get into this situation?" | Ronny asked, looking puzzled.

Cassie looked at Bo as if he'd just walked into the room. "You play baseball? That explains why you never seem to have a regular job."

Bo raised his palms. "Cassie, I—"

"Why would you keep that from me? I thought we'd told each other everything."

"I love baseball," Ronny said. "I used to play softball. And I used to watch the big games in Duffy's Tavern. What position do you play?"

"Shut the fuck up!" the gunman yelled. "Ay, ay, ay. *Mujeres estupidas.* If I was *jefe*, I sell drugs only. Woman never shut up."

Bo, palms in a raised position, stepped forward. He spoke in a soothing hushed voice. "*Amigo*, you must have a name."

"His name is Agapito," Cassie put in. "It means his mother loved him."

"What?" Ronny said. "How the hell do you know that?"

"Look, Agapito," Bo said. "Deal with me, okay?

These women are powerless and yes, they are stupid. You and I"--he swung his finger between the two of them--"we're men and we're in charge."

He unsnapped the concealed holster from inside the waistband of his jeans. "Here's my gun." He bent and laid it on the floor, slid it the few feet to the bandit. "You're right, you got me pegged. Here's my boot gun." He slid the smaller pistol across the floor. "Tell me what you need and how I can help you."

The gunman studied Bo through wary eyes, "You been taught well, Ranger. The one thing they did not teach you is we are smart and we don' give a damn what happens to us. That, my Ranger amigo, is bad for you and makes us that much more dangerous. You have homes to go back to. Nice lives. We have nothing. Death would be better for us. I welcome death, so save your psycho *mierda* and let me think."

Cassie, mirroring her occupational life, raised her hand high above her head, "Agapito, may I have permission to ask something? Is that's okay?"

"What you want now? You ask to bring the putas. I let you."

"What is this all about, Agapito? My sister and I moved here back in January when our father died. He owned this house, but we aren't involved in anything he did. We didn't even know him. He left us when we were little. If it's money you want, we don't have any and we don't do drugs."

"The *gringo viejo* is dead? I figured so. He got lucky. He would soon meet a very bad end. For long time he smuggle our women back into Texas. We thought he sell them or use them in trade, but no. He give them to church. I finally found the house, found the *túnel* and here we are."

He looked at Cassie. "You said no one would be here."

She shrugged. "Sorry. They got home early."

"You mean our dad was *actually* doing good?" Ronny said. "He was saving little girls like these from what, sex slavery?" She jabbed a finger at the bandit. "Tell you what, Buster. That gun may make you in charge of the situation, but it doesn't stop you from being an asshole."

Agapito raised his gun, pointed at Ronny. "I told you I shoot you—"

Everyone stiffened. Bo moved to touch Cassie.

"No. No touching," Agapito shouted.

"Hey, *amigo*, why don't you let the women go," Bo said calmly. "Take me. I'd make a grand prize for your boss. To take a Texas Ranger as hostage would bring you *mucho respeto*."

"Problems is all it would buy. No one wants to fight the state of Texas. No, I will give you the *putas*. I take the two *gringo* women back to Mexico with me. My *jefe* will love them, even if they are old. He use them as prizes."

Ronny didn't have to be told what that meant. She had to do something. "Old? I have you know we are anything but old!"

"And Bo," Cassie sobbed. "What's going to happen to Bo?"

"I have to kill your ranger, *señorita*."

"No, you can't. Don't you understand? He's someone I love."

"*El novio* is in dangerous line of work, *señorita.*
Do not worry. For you, I will kill him quickly.
They will never find his body or recognize it if
they do." He shrugged nonchalantly. "They may
give us some hell but without a body, it's anyone's
guess what happened. As you Americans like to say,
shit happens." He broke into laughter, "*Mierda pasa.*
Mierda pasa."

This dude is nuts! Ronny thought. She was intently
trying to figure a way out of this when she noticed
something she wasn't sure anyone else had seen. An
orange-red dot of light rested on Agapito the Bandit's
chest. She furtively glanced at the living room window
beside the fireplace and saw the unmistakable outline
of Tex holding a handgun.

Oh, my God. Does he have a laser, like in the movies?
She held her breath.

Before she could blink, an ear-piercing noise
coupled with breaking glass, ripped the silence. Then
a *thump*. A look of surprise on his face, the gunman
crumpled to his knees and fell forward.

Cassie collapsed in a dead faint.

Bo rushed to her side and dropped to his knees
beside her, lifted her to his lap. "Cassie, Cassie—"

"Cass? Cassie, are you alright?" Ronny bent down,
searching her sister's face.

Cassie's eyelids fluttered open. Ronny let out a
great breath. "Oh, my God, Cassie. You scared me to
death."

"Don't get up," Bo said to Cassie. "Just lie here for
a minute."

The front door crashed open. Tex dropped to the
living room floor and rolled across it, gun in hand.

Ronny walked over. "Okay, Chuck Norris, you can get up." She offered him a hand up. "You got the bad guy." He got to his feet and Ronny wrapped her arms around his big body. "And boy, am I glad you did. He was going to shoot me."

Tex walked over and studied Agapito's lifeless body, shoved his pistol into a shoulder holster. "Who is this? Anybody know?"

"Not yet," Bo answered.

"His name is Agapito," Cassie answered weakly.

The two strange girls were hugging each other and crying and jabbering in a language no one understood. The tension in the room had changed.

Bo got to his feet and helped Cassie stand. "You okay now, sweetheart?"

She nodded, staring down at Agapito. "He's so young." She wiped tears from her eyes. "I've never seen a dead person who wasn't in a coffin. Can—can we cover him up?"

"Absolutely," Bo said. He looked at Ronny.

"I'll get a towel. We don't have a spare sheet." She quickstepped toward the bathroom and returned with a bath towel.

"I'm going to have to report this as an active crime scene," Bo said, his arm around Cassie's waist. "Let's move outside."

Cassie nodded toward the strange girls. "Those girls—"

"I'll take care of it." Ronny walked over to where they were clinging to each other in the kitchen and coaxed them to go outside with her.

Bo picked up his weapons and put them away.

In the courtyard, hyped and talking rapidly, coming

down from an adrenaline rush, everyone congregated around the small wrought-iron table under the two palm trees. Bo seated Cassie in one of the two chairs. The gloaming cast everything in a golden glow and a light breeze touched their faces. A peaceful, beautiful end to a less than perfect day.

Bo slapped Tex on the shoulder. "Man, I didn't hear you drive up. I had no idea you were here but thank God you were. I think I was about to be fed to the coyotes or dropped into a vat of acid."

"I heard the gunfire when I was a couple hundred feet from the house," Tex replied. "I knew immediately what it was. I got out of my truck and ran the rest of the way. It damn near killed me."

Bo laughed. "Good shooting, pardner."

"I was breathing so hard I didn't trust my aim. I had to put the laser on."

"What kind of piece do you carry?"

"Colt 45 1911." He removed the pistol from its holster and handed it to Bo.

Bo fondled it. "Hm. I like the weight. And the chrome. And like the laser."

"It's a DLP Tactical."

Bo nodded, inspecting the laser mounted on the pistol's underside.

"Do you two have to have this conversation right now?" Ronny griped. "In case you haven't noticed, there's a dead body on our living room floor. You Texans may be comfortable with a body in the living room but it makes me nervous."

"I apologize," Bo said sincerely, "Let's just wait for the authorities."

Cassie thanked Tex, then turned to Bo. "Texas Ranger? We need to talk."

"Yes, ma'am. Let me make some calls first." He stepped away and pressed in numbers on his cell phone.

Ronny linked her arms in Tex's and leaned in, "Did you know Bo was a professional baseball player?"

Tex held her away. "You're serious? Are you in shock? Did you get hit by debris?" He pushed back her hair back to examine.

"Of course I'm serious. Agapito called him a Texas Ranger and—"

"I'll be damned," Tex said, staring at Bo's back. "Come to think of it, that's the first damn thing that has made any sense in a long time. Thinking back, it answers a lot of questions I had. Wow. I've lived close to the Border most of my life, but the only Texas Ranger I ever met was Joaquin Jackson out of Alpine."

"Who's that?" Ronny asked.

Tex shook his head. "Never mind. You and your sister might not realize it, but being a Texas Ranger is a bigger deal in Texas than being a baseball player."

Bo had finished his phone call and come back to where Ronny and Tex stood. "I'd like to know how you figure into this Bo, if that's even your real name," Tex said.

"Yes, sir. I'm Texas Ranger Beauregard McKinley Buckalew—"

Ronny tittered. Everyone stared at her.

"Sorry," she said. "It makes me laugh when he says that."

"I was assigned this case over a year ago," Bo went on. "I was to work undercover, get close to John Jennings and figure out exactly what and how he was doing what he did."

"And exactly what is it he did?" Tex asked.

"I finally learned the whole story just this week when I went to Austin. Jennings discovered that a tunnel that had been abandoned by one of the cartels years ago came from a poor neighborhood in Mexico, went under the river and came out on the backend of Jennings' property."

"Did you say under the river?" Tex asked. "Wow. That was a hell of an engineering feat."

"The cartels have money to burn. They can afford to hire the best engineers in the world. Anyway, Jennings approached Homeland Security and volunteered to use the tunnel to free victims who had been kidnapped and held in Mexico. The agency helped him reconstruct it and connect it to the back wall of his fireplace.

"I was always suspicious of the fireplace, but I couldn't figure it out. We didn't know if the few women who spoke up were telling the truth, if John was a helper or part of the problem. If there was a link to some Cartel, we were hoping he'd help bridge that link. His unexpected passing, of course, stalled our plan. In case you don't know it, we're at war with the drug cartels. If we don't get a grip on it, drug traffic from Mexico is going to be the end of the United States, not nuclear warfare."

"My dad was helping these poor girls?" Cassie said, her eyes brimming with tears that hadn't yet fallen,

"Reuniting families in the face of great risk? He was a hero and I never knew him."

"Indeed he was a hero," Bo said. "He was responsible for freeing many, many young girls and women. It was so incredibly dangerous to do what he did. Every woman he rescued put a bigger target on his back. We had a hard time believing anyone would take the risk to bring kidnapped women back home with no reward. We thought when he died the smuggling would end, too, but when those two girls showed up in Cassie and Ronny's living room, I was told to continue."

He turned to Cassie. "In Austin, I was ordered to come back here and put an end to everything. I was informed it's time to take over the premises, tear down some walls and open up that tunnel. I would basically be leaving you two homeless."

"Oh, my gosh," Cassie said. "The tunnel explains all the missing food right under our noses and we didn't have a clue."

"Now we're homeless!" Ronny said. "What more can this happy day bring?"

"There's a nice two-bedroom, two bath apartment above the café, you know," Tex said. "After Clay and Elena leave town, it'll be vacant."

"For the time being, I'll ask a deputy to take you ladies to Harlingen and you can get a room in a motel," Bo said. "Paid for by the State of Texas, of course."

"Don't forget we need to talk," Cassie reminded him.

"Oh, I haven't forgotten, Cassie. I haven't forgotten."

EPILOGUE

WITH RESEARCH HAVING indicated the little orange adobe house was well over two hundred years old, the State of Texas laid claim to it and the surrounding five acres through eminent domain and offered Cassie and Ronny the market price for it. Due to the will's provisions, this presented a problem.

Meanwhile, homeless, the sisters were forced to move into the apartment above the café.

Paxton Atwater approached a district judge and discussed the unusual circumstances of the Jennings sisters' inheritance. The judge determined that Cassie and Ronny were being forced to leave the property due to no fault of their own. Though they still owned 75 of the original 80 acres, thus saving the pasture where the four longhorn steers lived, caring for them in the future would be difficult. Atwater discussed the Future Farmers of America being given custody of the cattle to be used as an educational subject for children. The judge thought that a good idea. Cassie and Ronny agreed, with the proviso that they could not be sold for slaughter.

The Judge vacated the will, including the provision requiring the sisters to wait a year for access to the safety deposit box.

In a formal meeting at the bank that included the presence of the bank manager as well as a representative from the court as witnesses, Atwater opened the box. They discovered a stack of unopened letters and cards mailed to their mother in Tonawilla, New York. They also fund a brown envelope containing a cashier's check for a million dollars. Cassie and Ronny both gasped and stared at each other. What else could they do when they were speechless? They needed a financial advisor immediately.

In reading the letters found in the safe deposit box, Cassie and Ronny learned that their father had not abandoned them because he wanted nothing to do with them. Their mother had kept him away. She had not wanted to follow him to Texas herself and feared he might lure their daughters.

Meanwhile, the State of Texas collapsed the tunnel with strategically placed dynamite, repaired the damage to the house and restored the whole place to how it had looked in its beginning. When they finished, it was more primitive than when Cassie and Ronny had first walked into it with the bathroom being removed altogether. It was marked off with a historical marker and fenced off.

Bo, his undercover assignment completed, returned to his home base in Marfa. He returned to Los Tropicos to visit Cassie often.

The café continued to be busy. Customer loyalty seemed not to have faltered. The diners were amused and entertained by two young Yankee women who had never been out of New York owning a Mexican food café and cooking Mexican food in South Texas.

Tex completed Buds & Suds and opened it. On weekends, more customers than the small space would hold spilled over into the cafe. The café sold many, many plates of spicy nachos.

At the end of the school year in Tonawilla, Cassie obtained her certificate for teaching in Texas schools, but put off applying for a teaching job. She had bonded with the two pitiful captive women, who, she learned, came from Russia. They had been shunted from their homeland to Massachusetts, to South America, to Mexico. Cassie's instinct for nurturing and teaching couldn't be denied. She negotiated with the State of Texas to train them for café and restaurant work.

Though the women's first language was Russian and they spoke very little English, Cassie soldiered through, taught them basic English and put them to work in the café, the name of which had been changed from Elena's to Café dos Hermanos.

Bo missed Cassie in his life and his absence wore on her, too. She soon found herself wearing an engagement ring and planning a wedding.

In his quiet moments, Tex took up learning to play the guitar. Often, he could be heard strumming and Ronny could be heard singing *El Rancho Grande* in the café kitchen.

Life in Texas was good.

ALSO BY DIXIE CASH

You Can Have My Heart, but Leave My Dog Alone
I Can't Make You Love Me, but I Can Make You Leave
Our Red Hot Romance is Leaving Me Blue
Curing the Blues with a New Pair of Shoes
Don't Make Me Choose Between You and My Shoes
I Gave You My Heart, but You Sold It Online
My Heart May Be Broken, but My Hair Still Looks
Great
Since You're Leaving Anyway, Take Out the Trash

www.ingramcontent.com/pod-product-compliance
Lightning Source LLC
Chambersburg PA
CBHW072226170626
46813CB00003B/1112